BIFOCAL
CURIOUS TALES & THEIR REFLECTIONS

Published in Canada by Engen Books, St. John's, NL.

Library and Archives Canada Cataloguing in Publication

Title: Bifocal : curious tales & their reflections / Andrew Peacock & Kaleigh Middelkoop.
Names: Peacock, Andrew (Veterinarian), author. | Middelkoop, Kaleigh, photographer.
Description: Stories by Andrew Peacock ; photography by Kaleigh Middelkoop.
Identifiers: Canadiana (print) 20210244771 | Canadiana (ebook) 2021024478X | ISBN 9781774780466
  (softcover) | ISBN 9781774780473 (PDF)
Classification: LCC PS8631.E217 B54 2021 | DDC C813/.6—dc23

Distributed by:
Engen Books
www.engenbooks.com
submissions@engenbooks.com

First mass market printing: November 2021

Cover Image: Kaleigh Middelkoop
Watercolours: Ellen Curtis

FOR PETRA + ALWIN

BIFOCAL

ANDREW PEACOCK & KALEIGH MIDDELKOOP

Andrew

Dedication

For Charlotte, Winston and the view from the hill.

Welcome to Bifocal

Bifocal is not intended to be just a series of stories illustrated by photography. This work is a synergistic effort where the pictures provide new insights into the stories which in turn illuminate the photography. The images of Bifocal do not merely retell the stories but attempt to capture a feeling or explore a concept or emotion from the tales. The writing interprets the photographs in much the same manner.

Some of what follows are straightforward descriptions of life. Other stories may be structured in the form of a letter, pure dialogue, or constrained writing. "I Will Not Use Those Words" is restricted to words of one syllable and "Rule of Thirds" has three sections each consisting of exactly 900 words and a three-word title. The photographs range from the natural to the surreal, often using complex props and digital photo manipulation.

Dig in.

Ten Hard Ones

Perhaps I worry too much about making the right choices when I shop. I am walking down the cereal aisle in the grocery store looking for some *instant* oatmeal when a familiar song comes over the tinny speakers hidden up in the ceiling. I recognize the tune. It's a Canadian singer and she's telling us all about the irony of rain coming down on someone's wedding day.

The *enormity* of my oatmeal search and its attendant problems overwhelm me. First off, the oatmeal isn't instant - instant means happening immediately. It takes some time for the oatmeal to cook, so it might be very fast oatmeal, but it's not instant. I'll have to find another way to describe the oatmeal. Next, I realize that there is nothing bad or evil about my shopping expedition. Enormity doesn't mean large or ponderous, that's enormousness. Enormity means very bad or evil. I picked the wrong word again.

This shopping trip and story are off to a bad start. What I need is some kind of *panacea*, but no, that's not the right word. I'm only looking for a cure for this misuse of words and inability to pick up provisions. A panacea is something that cures everything. It's common to use it to describe a complete cure of one thing but the word has a much narrower definition.

My difficulty with choosing the groceries and words is *chronic*, I've been looking for the right foodstuffs and words for a long time. I got that one right. Despite the way it's often used, chronic doesn't necessarily relate to a bad situation. So I put the oatmeal into my cart and move over to the fruit section. We're low on apples and I pick up ten.

On the way to the cash one of my apples rolls out of the cart and is moistly ruined beneath my front wheel. My fruit selection has been *decimated*. As the apple has its insides squeezed, I can feel the complaints that I should have lost nine of the apples. But decimate comes from the Latin term for the punishment where one in every ten men was killed. To decimate is to lose one in ten.

If you'd like to *refute* this meaning of decimate, you had better have a dictionary with you. Refute doesn't just mean to say something is wrong, it means to prove something is wrong with evidence to the contrary. I think I'm ready to check out now, this shopping is exhausting.

My eyes *literally* pop out of my head when I see the sign at the checkout counter. Well, no, not literally - if they literally popped out they would make a mess something like the apple did on the floor.

The sign says "Ten items or *less*" and that's just wrong. Less means a smaller amount of something that can't be counted. The sign should say "Ten items or fewer." I can go home with my very fast cooking oatmeal and decide to put less milk in, but if I decrease the number of bagels I accompany it with, this would be fewer.

The checkout girl looks *disinterested*, but no, that's wrong too. She's really uninterested if my hunch is right. If she was disinterested, she would be independent, an unbiased judge of what is going on here. I think she may not be thrilled to be working today, but she will have opinions on how much the apples cost and whether I should pay for the one that was eviscerated on the tiles.

I offer up my credit card and have time to squeeze in the *ultimate* word. That doesn't mean it's the best one, just the last in a series. My list has been filled and I'm heading home for a rest.

HOLES

I think you would like the new house. It's in another town - I had to move away. Of course it's smaller, but it works for me.

There is an enormous hole in the centre, the absolute heart of my new home - no not home - house. I got a good price on the place because the previous owners started work that they never finished. In the course of renovations they removed a colossus of a chimney, a dirty conglomeration of bricks and mortar. And then when the chimney came out, there was nothing there to take its place.

I stood on a chair and looked up into that empty space. You can see the inside of the roof and the intricate arrangement of wood that holds everything together. There are beams that run across the room wrapped in insulation and then strapping, fibreboard and a tiled ceiling. Someone must have decided they didn't like the look of the tiles because there is a whole other layer under all of this. There is more strapping that holds up the spackled Gyproc that makes up the ceiling that's visible from below. You would have liked all this complicated layering.

That's a lot of material and weight pulling down on the structure of the house. But I suppose it's a good idea. The rest of the building is solid and I'm not worried that anything will fall apart. Other than that hole, there is lots between me and the outside, between me and the cold, between me and whatever is out there.

I don't think I can describe that place where the chimney was as a vacuum, it's nothing. A vacuum is a space with nothing in it. There's not even a space there, nothing to be filled, nothing that can be filled. Just emptiness.

The old house was just too painful to live in anymore. Last year it was a place full of joy. Our children were born and raised there. A menagerie of dogs shared our space. Noise and laughter were our constant companions.

I sold the old house. The kids were divided on this. They all said it was full of memories, but they couldn't agree on what that really meant. Some of them insisted we should save the place as some kind of memorial to everything that went on there. But that house was never really ours. We don't genuinely own anything. Not land, not buildings, and certainly not the past.

The agent that sold the old house is the same one that found me the new place. He is a guy that I would have pointed out to you. First time he came by he had a classy scarf, long wild blond hair and he smelled nice. Funny that I even remember that, because there's no lust left in me. It got smashed out like the air from a soccer ball run over by a transport truck.

I don't think either one of us would have predicted that. We talked many times about what we would do if one of us was left alone. We always insisted we'd keep having fun, we'd start over and not let the past interfere with the future. If it was you left, I'd want you to carry on - find someone new, enjoy life again. We couldn't conceive of the possibility that happiness depended on both of us being around.

One trip across town seemingly protected by a ton of metal, and all those ideas were gone like flash paper. It should have been the safest journey imaginable. All it took was one big truck coming in fast at a right angle to change everything about our world.

Metal smashing into metal, glass shattering – shattering windshields and lives into shards. A big bang louder than a hammer on the side of your head and since then a silence so intense it screams.

The kids are grown and away. They visit, and even though I need them like I never did before, we don't have much to say when we're together. Their presence is awkward and there seems to be nothing to talk about. I can't stand it when they're gone but I can't wait for them to leave.

Maybe what I miss the most are the sandwiches. Every day you made my lunch. Not many men do that, but every morning you put together my sandwiches. Always two slices of ancient grains bread, just the right amount of butter, sandwich meat, lettuce and a little mayonnaise. The meals you prepared were perfect.

Every day at work I would take out my sandwich and see the little bite you took out of the corner. We never talked about that. You never asked me if I noticed and I never told you how much it meant to me. I think we both knew.

I don't eat sandwiches anymore. For a while they were the only thing that was left without a hole. The holes in my life have hurt me as much as anything ever could, but in a way, I still need some holes. I tell myself and the kids it has to be this way at least for a while.

I'm afraid you would be disappointed if you saw where I spend my nights. My bed's where the chimney used to be. I sleep best when I can see the moon. For a while every month it has a hole bitten out of the side and I just wish I could pull that beautiful white shining moon down into my empty space.

We always said we wouldn't live like this if life worked out the way it has, but it's the best I can do right now.

A Stranger to Myself

Let me call myself Edmund Allan. That isn't my name, but for the telling of my story, it works well. My real life is much-covered by the media. If you live in the right part of the world, you will have seen me on television and in the newspapers. My position in life is one that interests the masses and their impression of me is important to my continued success.

Anyone watching from the outside must surely be certain that I love public attention. For me, this constant scrutiny is but a necessary thorn in my existence. My reputation and prominence are both the cause and effect of my success. However, my true passion in life lies in other places.

Cartooning has interested me since I was a young boy. I continue to draw to this day. My work has never been published, but producing this art is important to me. It took some time to realize that my cartoons were an attempt to represent who and what I really am.

My success in life has come from my ability to know the wants and needs of those around me. From early on I understood that in order to clearly see others, I must first be able to see something of myself. Like many who write, paint and sing, at the core, my work is about trying to understand me.

One of the harshest realities of life is the way in which we are all condemned to be strangers to ourselves. It's a cruel irony that the being we inhabit is the one that we can never perceive. My wife is the person closest to me in the world and I know what every part of her looks like. From the front and back, I have spent hours investigating every aspect of her being.

Although I see myself in the mirror every morning and have watched hours of footage and seen thousands of still pictures of myself, I've never really looked directly at me. A mirror is not reality; photos and television programs are even further removed from the truth.

A few months ago, I went for lunch at an outdoor café near my office. I wore sunglasses to protect my privacy and revelled in the chance to be in a

public place and still relatively undisturbed.

The food was superb. I had a salad made of crispy lettuce with strawberries and dates. The dressing was inventive and perfectly complemented the other flavours. Because my lunch was minimal, I allowed myself the luxury of a small serving of crème brulee to finish.

I was just scraping out the inside of the ramekin when I heard a female voice call out my first name. Like my real name, Edmund is just unusual enough that I always assume that I am being addressed when I hear it called.

I was at the same time disappointed and intrigued that I was being disturbed during a rare chance to be alone. Still, the voice was alluring, and I was curious to see who it belonged to. My male vanity couldn't help speculating that I still had the position and appearance to attract female admirers.

When I turned my head towards the sound, my name repeated, and I saw a very attractive young redheaded woman walking in my direction. The smile on her face was the type that, in my experience, is only afforded to close acquaintances.

I was puzzling over this expression on someone completely unknown to me when she stopped short at a table about ten meters from mine.

She leaned in and kissed Edmund (I had to assume this was his name) on the cheek and took a seat across from him. She faced me and all I could see of Edmund was his back.

I couldn't draw my eyes away from her. I have always been faithful to my wife, but there are people that I cannot help looking at. Most of these are women. My wife knows this aspect of my character and is undisturbed by it. She knows where my allegiance lies and is unworried by my appreciation of feminine beauty.

Edmund and the redhead finished before me and after paying the bill they got up and left with their backs in my direction. They didn't hold hands, but their proximity as they moved suggested an easy familiarity.

As I lay in bed that night, the events at the café came back to my mind. It surprised me that my thoughts turned more to Edmund than his comely companion. There was something about the man that kept twisting through my consciousness.

Although my name isn't common, I had encountered other men called Edmund before. Still, there was something beyond this that bothered me. As I tried to bring his image back to my mind, it occurred to me that there were similarities in our appearance.

Like me, he was a slim man. His hair was about the same colour and had the same look of neglect. His clothes were much like what I would choose to wear, and I estimated that he would be about the same height as me.

The more I reflected, the more I regretted that I had not paid more attention to the man. Throughout the meal, my mind was focused on his companion. As trivial as these concerns may seem, they kept me from sleeping for a number of hours.

The next morning, I began to plot how I could find Edmund again and satisfy myself that our shared name and similar appearance was of no significance. As I searched for a way to reacquaint myself with him, I realized that I had almost no useful information. A first name is little help in tracking down anyone. All I knew was that he had spent one lunch hour at the café near my office.

For the next two weeks, I went to this same establishment every day at lunch. I gradually increased the time I spent looking for Edmund until I was usually there from 11:30 to 1:30. Because of the prominence of my position, no one complained about my extended lunch breaks.

Eventually, I decided that my quest was at once foolish and unattainable. I stopped haunting the café and was satisfied that there was no reason to continue with my obsession.

It was a week later when I saw Edmund again. It was in the parking garage that it seems we shared. I was just locking my own car when he walked by. This time I saw him in unobstructed profile. Although I've never really seen myself from the side, it was apparent that this was the same man and that there was a definite similarity between his face and mine.

I followed him from a respectful distance along the street and into a building that was close to where I work. After he entered an elevator at the end of the lobby I stood back and watched the numbers above the door. As he was the only one to get in the elevator and there was no disruption in its ascent, I could logically conclude that he got off on the fifth floor.

The directory board by the reception desk indicated that there was only one company at that location, a computer graphics firm called Unreality.

When I got back to my own office, I did a search of Unreality's website and found that indeed there was a man called Edmund involved. He was the president and his last name was Allan. There was no history or description of him, but there was a photograph and I was certain he looked exactly like me.

I did another online search to find more information about my apparent twin. There were pages about my position and history but not a mention of the second Edmund Allan. Not even his listing on the Unreality website came up on any search engine I tried.

That night I told my wife the story of my strange discovery and was somewhat disappointed when her only reaction was to laugh and suggest I had a vivid imagination. She recognized my frustration at her response and agreed to look at the picture on the Unreality page. I could hardly believe it when she shrugged her shoulders and suggested that the man didn't look anything like me.

I downloaded the picture of Edmund Allan, enlarged it to a full screen view and set my laptop up in front of the bathroom mirror. For nearly an hour I traced each line of his face, the set of his eyes, the angle of his chin and the contours of his lips. Every feature seemed to line up precisely with the image of myself in the mirror.

Despite my certainty, I decided to abandon any attempt to show my wife how much she had underappreciated the similarities. Even without her support, there was no way I could leave this situation alone. I decided that I had to observe Mr. Allan more carefully.

The next day, I left the office a half hour before normal lunch time and walked to the Unreality building. It took twenty minutes of leaning against a wall with a nonchalant newspaper, but Edmund Allan finally appeared. This time he had a younger man with him. I followed them to a restaurant and sat at the next table.

The waiter came to me first and I ordered the daily special of French onion soup. Allan ordered the same meal.

For the first time, I was able to hear him speak. He didn't have much to say but carried on polite conversation with his colleague. My initial reaction was relief that this man who looked so much like me seemed sophisticated and well-mannered.

As his discussion continued, I began to carefully analyze the pattern and tone of his speech. His voice was pleasant, and he had absolutely no accent. I was close enough to follow the full conversation and was impressed with his opinions and ability to explain them. Even when their discussion veered into abstract realms, I could clearly follow all of his reasoning.

A thought began to develop in my mind that there was something very familiar about his voice. I tested out the concern that he might sound like me by calling for the waiter and saying a few words about how much I liked the soup. I couldn't hear any clear relationship between our voices, and this gave me some comfort.

Perhaps it was just out of boredom that I took out my phone and recorded some of Edmund Allan's speech.

Back at my office, after the excellent meal, I took out my phone and listened to my recording. Again, there was something very familiar about everything I heard. It struck me nearly an hour later that this voice did sound like me, but it wasn't the me that I heard from inside my head. When I found an interview with myself online and played it, it was clear that Allan sounded exactly like I did when someone else was listening.

This revelation disturbed me enough that I began following Allan every day over lunch and even tried tailing him to his residence after work. Somehow, I could never manage to stay close enough to him to find out exactly where he lived. I made great efforts to be in my car when he got to our parking garage, but I was never able to keep with him on his drive home.

I became more and more reckless in my reconnaissance, sitting near him for almost every workday lunch. One time when we went to a restaurant with a short wait for seating, I was bold enough to sit on the chair next to him in the waiting area.

As soon as I sat down, I worried that Allan would confront me about this now impossible-to-miss stalking that I was engaged in. He looked my way and nodded as I sat down, but his manner was that of someone seeing another person for the very first time. There was absolutely no evidence of any recognition on his part.

I couldn't understand how this man didn't see how much alike we were. To test his recognition of the strangeness of our similarity, I made a point of calling the waiter over and telling him that a friend of mine might have called with a message. I clearly pointed out that my name was Edmund Allan. The other Edmund Allan showed no response.

Sitting this close to him I also noticed that the man had no odour. I consider myself a careful observer of the world around me and take some pride in my ability to distinguish different smells. I can tell if my wife has worn a shirt of mine even days after she has done it. This man left absolutely no olfactory trail.

I began to worry about my sanity as thoughts came up that perhaps this man really was me. The idea was preposterous, but I couldn't ignore the evidence that we were precisely the same.

His manner, his choice of clothing, his appearance and his voice were exact mirrors of everything from my existence.

The only thing I could see different about the two of us was his relationship with the redheaded woman that I had seen at our first encounter. About once or twice a week this beautiful girl would meet Edmund Allan for lunch.

My obsession with our similarities led me to an irrational anger when I saw the two of them together. Somehow, I would have been happier to see Allan meeting with my wife for these meals.

The final disturbing occurrence in my encounters with Edmund Allan was on my birthday. I followed him to a more upscale restaurant than he had used for any previous meals. Once again, I took a table near his and again, he showed no evidence of recognizing me.

I ordered first and he waved off the waiter when she came to his table. Fifteen minutes after we arrived, the redheaded woman came in and sat beside him. Perhaps I shouldn't have been surprised when she pulled out a small package and effused about how wonderful a man he was and that he deserved a little extra attention on his birthday.

They leaned forward from their seats and kissed. He opened the package and made a big fuss about the Rolex watch that she had given him. He protested that the gift was too expensive and looked genuinely embarrassed.

I was flustered enough that I couldn't finish my meal, and unlike every other time I had watched Allan eat, I left before him.

At home that night, my wife could see there was something wrong. As disturbing as the affair had been, I couldn't bring myself to tell her the details. She had dismissed my initial recognition of the strange relationship between me and Allan and I was certain that all of my stories would be met with derision.

Still, I needed reassurance and comfort. I asked her if she would come over beside me on the couch so that we could just sit together quietly.

I reached around her shoulder and pulled her in close. This was the one place in the world that everything seemed sane. I knew who I was and where I fit into the world.

She reached up and reassuringly held my hand.

"That's a lovely watch. Where did you get it?"

FREEDOM

Gerard wasn't sure he could remember the first time someone hit him. By the time he started school, his father had moved out. Although he had no distinct memories, he was sure that the old man had been physical with him. The violence from home and the teachers at school subtly blended together.

Learning was always a challenge for Gerard. He never had encouragement from home and he often fell asleep during classes. The other kids made fun of him and called him stupid. At first he would turn his back and get away as fast as he could. Then one time, four boys cornered him outside the school and started into a contest to see who could say the meanest thing about Gerard. A part of him broke when a tall skinny kid called his mother a drunk. He'd said the same thing quite a few times himself, but no one else had the right to speak of his mother that way. He hit the kid hard enough to knock out a tooth and the other three ran off fast.

Gerard learned that he didn't need to hit anyone to be left alone. All he had to do was clench his fist and rub it with the other hand. He soon joined forces with a couple of tough kids and no one bothered them or even talked to them.

When he was sixteen, three of them robbed the local convenience store. On their way out, the store manager and a couple of bystanders took up the chase. His buddies knew that their getaway depended on not being the slowest offender. One of them wasn't quite as fast as Gerard, but a well-placed foot put Gerard down on his face. The vigilantes beat him just a little and he ended up with a short sentence at the boys' home.

That was the end of Gerard's time in school. When he got out he started drinking, and time went slowly with no friends and no work. His social worker found him an apartment in a rundown building. Things sort of spiraled down for Gerard. The whole place smelled bad enough that he felt no inspiration to keep his room clean. The garbage piled up in the apartment to the point that it was hard to walk inside the front door. The fact that he started to smell as bad as the room made it difficult for an already antisocial man to make friends.

Gerard found a bicycle abandoned on the street and started going everywhere on it. He soon became a fixture in the community, the guy with watery blue eyes and greasy hair riding around with a cigarette hanging from his lips. The bike gave him mobility. It was easier to get to the grocery store, so he started picking up fresher supplies every few days. The change in food inspired him to cook a little more and clean up his kitchen. Soon everything scattered on the floor was out on the street, ready for the garbage truck to take away.

His cleaning efforts produced a large pile of trash, so he stood by the curb and waited for the truck. When they pulled up, he started throwing the big plastic bags before the workers had a

chance to tell him he had too much garbage. He expected the guys on the truck to yell at him and say he'd put out more than allowed, but they slapped him on the back and thanked him for his help.

After that he called out to the truck every time he passed them on his bicycle. The garbage men always had a friendly wave for him.

One day the driver called him over as he drove by. One of the guys on the truck had moved on to the city and they needed someone else for the job. Gerard started right away working three days a week.

He enjoyed the new structure in his life. Mondays, Tuesdays and Thursdays he would be out of bed by seven and ride his bicycle to the town depot. His spot was on the back of the truck with his feet on the running board and one arm holding the chrome bar that ran down from the frame of the box.

Gerard soon developed a feel for tensing and relaxing as the truck started and stopped. He jumped down just before the vehicle came to a halt and scooped up the bags on the curb. He could have never guessed the freedom of fresh air and exercise that would come with loading a garbage truck.

He started to gain friends. There was an elderly lady who was always just a little late for the truck. She would yell out "yoo hoo" from her front porch as the truck pulled up and rush inside to put together a final collection of refuse. Gerard took to meeting her at the door and toting the bag to the truck. On the Thursday just before Christmas the woman had her garbage ready at the curb and was standing with a capped paper cup full of coffee for Gerard. He made the drink last his whole shift as he dexterously completed his rounds.

It was just a week after that run that his manager called him in to let him know that his job was gone. The mayor's nephew was back from work on the oil rigs in Alberta and wanted some work over the winter. That night someone stole Gerard's bicycle from his yard.

He drank more than he had for many months and in a stupor, took a knife from the kitchen block and headed out for the mayor's convenience store. Although his waving of the weapon in the store looked more like a convulsion than a concerted attack, the girl at the counter was quick to hand him the cash from the till.

Three kids looking at magazines in the back were enthusiastic witnesses when the police arrived. No one knew the robber's name, but everyone agreed that it was the blue-eyed guy from the garbage truck that always had a cigarette hanging from his mouth.

The police soon identified Gerard and it seemed no more than a formality of justice that he ended up at the prison farm for four months.

At first Gerard cursed his impatience. A moment of anger and despair had perhaps ruined his life. His mind gradually changed as he settled into existence at the farm. The meals were reliable and they were always good. He had to work, but there was choice - he could cook, do janitorial service or look after the animals. Gerard chose the animals and soon he was milking cows twice a day. There were only a dozen cows, so the work wasn't hard, but it gave him a reason to get up every morning.

Gerard didn't really have friends at the farm, but there was an old guy that he ate many of his meals with. Max had about a third of his teeth left and his major skill in life seemed to be his ability to do nothing. When the warden asked Max which job he wanted he told him he didn't want to work. They put him on kitchen cleanup and although he would carry a mop around, no ever saw him actually do anything with it. Max didn't read and he didn't play cards. He seemed happy to watch everyone else get on with their lives.

They talked at meals and Max was happy to outline his life philosophy to Gerard. In his mind, the world was unfair. He had tried as a young man to accomplish things, but there was always some spot of bad luck or unfair interference that blocked his way. In his late twenties, Max decided that trying was for fools and he spent the rest of his time doing as little as possible. He still knew what a good life was and he was willing to put in the minimum required to keep himself in comfort. An example of his minimal effort was the way to stay warm in the winter. Every year in late November, Max would stand in front of a jewelry store and throw a rock through the window. It was important not to have a gun, that might get you into the pen and that was certainly not a comfortable life. But if you just stood there and waited for the police or maybe yelled and waved a knife around when they came, you could be guaranteed a warm, well-fed winter at the farm.

By the time his sentence was up, Gerard was a little disappointed to leave. Because he no longer had a bicycle, he decided to move into the city. His government cheque was enough to get him a dirty, cold apartment and there was almost enough left over to eat. His meals were simple, usually something out of a can that he heated up on his hot plate. There was no oven or real stove in his place.

During the summer he spent his days walking the city streets. There was always much to see and in the evenings there was romance and violence better than anything on the TV. The days on the garbage truck were a distant memory and he had no desire to find work.

He started drinking again and soon his mornings were spent under the covers nursing a sore head. His strolling routine shifted later into the days. Before long, he wasn't on the streets until late in the afternoon.

As the summer dropped down into fall temperatures, life became more difficult. It wasn't comfortable to sit in the park for long periods of time. He looked at the homeless men and hoped that he would never become one of them, wrapped in a blanket on a chilly day. Gerard had some pride left and the discomfort of the cold weighed heavily on his mind.

It was early December before the temperature dropped precipitously. On a Thursday night Gerard found himself wandering the main downtown street. Even though it was only seven o'clock, the sky was as black as it could get above a modern city. Snow swirled down in a moderate wind that was romantic to some and almost unbearable to others. Families were out with their fashionably bulky jackets, peering through storefront windows. Gerard wondered why anyone with a warm house would be on the streets on a night like this.

The Hudson's Bay store had the most spectacular display of any of the establishments in the city. There was a model train running through valleys between snow-topped mountains. A city more innocent than the one he stood in was lit with minilights. Groups of children caroled and friendly dogs looked on.

Gerard joined a group ogling the scene. As he watched the onlookers it struck him that people were looking at different things. The children and the more innocent among the crowd could only see the display. There were others, mostly the best dressed among the throng who were obviously seeing something else. The way that they straightened their hats or shifted their jackets so the buttons ran symmetrically down their torsos made it clear they were seeing their reflections. No doubt some were even seeing both and wondering how their lives were better or worse than the display before them.

Gerard shivered and wondered if anyone else was watching the same thing he was. All he could see was the glass.

PAINT

The mustard yellow of their rented house prejudiced the colour that the morning sun lent to the gravel and weeds of the front garden. Cadmore strolled out with coffee in hand and settled on a bench under a weather-worn maple tree. A pretty pigtailed girl looked up at him through her bangs as she flitted by the house on her way to the school bus. He absentmindedly sipped from his mug without returning her glance.

Comfortably on the bench, he pulled the rolled scribbler from his back pocket and the pen from behind his ear. Then he sat and stared straight ahead as his coffee chilled. His immobility lasted the fifteen minutes it took for Brian to scurry back from his errand.

"Dad, Dad, I've got your baguette and a pain au chocolat for me. There was a big crowd at the shop this morning."

"Thanks, Brian. You're getting big, running off for breakfast by yourself. It's a great help."

"Dad, Mme. Beauchamp gave me a piece of chocolate too. I think it's because I knocked over the new lady's bags when I ran in. She looks like Mom, Dad. She had paint all over her shirt and she stunk of turpentine."

Cadmore rubbed his hand through Brian's hair. It startled him when his son conjured up memories of Laura. It had been four years since... well, since they had come from Canada to this small town in southern France. The corners of his eyes creased as he thought of her messy studio and the wildly coloured paintings she created.

They ate their breakfasts in silence. The chocolate kept Brian too occupied to speak but didn't stop him from sprinting down the road to harass the local pigeons. When they were finished, Brian moved back into the house to read his day's lessons. His father would come in from time to time for a break from the wind and to check on the boy's progress.

Between his trips into the house, Cadmore sat on the bench and watched the shade patterns on the gravel shift. His scribbler sat on his knee and his pen moved from his side to his lips to the edge of the page. Not one word was written.

The next morning unfolded much like the one before and the one before that. Brian went to the shop and Cadmore sat on the bench.

"Dad, the lady was there again! She paid for our stuff."

"Brian, I gave you enough cash for that food. We don't need charity, we have enough money for what we need."

"Where does the money come from? You're supposed to be a writer, Dad. What have you written since we came here?"

"You'd better get back in your room, Brian. I'm going to run over to the store and pay that woman back."

Brian scuttled inside and Cadmore made his way to the shop. Even though it was only a short walk from their house, he had not been by the establishment for over six months. As he crested the low hill beyond the church he noticed the new sign above the door of the bakery. It was plain and the letters were just a little crooked, but it wasn't ugly. He reflected that he needed to get out more when he missed alterations in a village that changed as glacially as this place.

"Morning, Mme. Beauchamp. Do you know the woman who paid for Brian's stuff this morning?"

"Ah, yes, the young painter. She left just a while ago. You know that place just past Jean Marie's vineyard where all the artists are? She's away from the rest a bit, the farthest one out."

"Merci, Mme. Beauchamp."

Cadmore strode back to the house and checked that Brian was reading. He pulled his bicycle from the small shed out back and pedalled through the town. It had been some time since he had used the bicycle and his calves complained as he struggled up the hill and past the white stuccoed church. The road levelled out and he smiled at the vigorous head kink from his neighbour who passed him in his comically small imitation of a pickup truck. Two men smoking and leaning on a fence waved and offered "bonjours" as he puffed by.

The cobblestones ended at the same time as the houses. A goat on a rope stepped up on a fence board and twisted his head as he stared with oddly rectangular pupils. When Cadmore caught sight of the small building at the end of the artists' colony he stepped off his bike and leaned on the handlebars. What was he thinking? How could he barge into the studio and confront this woman? What would he say? As he turned his bicycle around he thought he would be better getting back at his writing.

He spent the rest of the day sitting on his bench. For the last four years he had sat in the same space, thinking about his novel and writing nothing. This time he didn't think about the book.

The next morning Cadmore decided he would go to the shop and talk to the artist woman. He told Brian to sit on the bench and wait for his breakfast. The air was only slightly chilled by the breeze coming in across the fields and Brian's father felt good moving so early in the day. The strutting pigeons seemed to offer encouragement at every step along the way.

Looking up, he collided with a woman hustling out the shop door. He excused himself and looked straight into the bluest eyes he had ever seen. They both smiled and with a quick "pardon," she was out the door. He turned to watch her paint-splattered jeans skip down the road.

In a trance, he moved to the counter. "I see you've met our new artist," said Mme. Beauchamp. "She's a beauty, isn't she? And this woman can paint, I have a work of hers hanging myself."

Cadmore turned and stumbled back to his house. She was beautiful, and she was an artist. It was foolish, but he knew that something about the girl had taken hold of him.

Back at their bench, Brian sighed as he saw his father return without their breakfast.

"Sit down, Dad. Do I have to do everything for you? I'll run back and get some food."

Cadmore smiled absently and pulled out his scribbler. By the time Brian returned he had two pages filled. He put down the baguette his son handed him and continued to write.

Back in the small studio, the woman had returned home. She unscrewed the top from a Coke bottle, opened the bag of chips she had brought from the shop and started work on another sign. This time it was for the small engine repair place in the village. It was hard work painting signs, but as challenging as it might be, it was a change from the house painting she normally did.

A Matter of Balance

The stadium is packed and the air is filled with an expectant buzz that is audible over the southern blues rock that blasts out from the tons of speakers suspended above the front of the stage. The lights go down and there is a shriek from the front section of the floor. A lone bass drum beats out a slow tattoo and somber blue lights slowly increase in intensity and sweep the front of the stage.

The excitement in the crowd increases palpably as the beat gets louder and slower. The sound stops suddenly, the lights flash brilliant yellow and there he is, standing with his right hand raised straight above his head. The audience erupts into a roar that might be a scream or a cheer.

His arm comes down and the band crashes into that song that sold millions over a decade ago. The intensity of the sound waves sends a tremor through his body, but the real effect on him is the movement he sees in the audience. He can't make out that much through the lights, but there is a sense that everyone is travelling upwards. If they weren't standing before that first note, they all are now, and the ones who were standing are just a little more upright and straining for the sky.

He sings and the first few notes are rote. This is his job and he's done it a thousand times before. Sometimes it's to an empty rehearsal room and sometimes it's to tens of thousands of the faithful. It takes him until the second verse to really feel the love and yearning from down below.

There are probably five thousand in this arena. He played much bigger shows in the past, but he knows everyone in the building is here for him. Tickets are expensive and that keeps anyone away who doesn't like him or is even ambivalent. Even the tough guys that are here because of their girls are on his side.

The song ends with four unison crashes from guitars, bass and drums and he drops dramatically to his knees. He closes his eyes and pauses to take in the adulation that washes across the room. This is what he's here for.

There is a slight drop in energy after the first song. People sit, but it's obvious they are still under his spell. About an hour in, the band starts into the slow song that was a monster hit five years back. The lights are hushed and immediately the floor fills with points of illumination. Back when the song was everywhere it would have been lighters filling the darkness but now it's cell phones. There's something a little tacky about the atmosphere, but he can still feel the emotion. Couples hold each other and sway to the rhythm. Everyone sings along with the chorus.

The last four songs are all minor hits. The crowd knows every word. They sing and bellow until they are hoarse. The final song ends with perhaps too many repetitions of the last chord. The drummer climbs down from his riser and the band locks arms and bow to the crowd like under-rehearsed Rockettes. They leave the stage in single file.

The lights stay down and the audience starts to clap. The sound is small at first, but it grows as the people become impatient for more. They love him and would do anything for him, but they've paid good money for the show and he owes them just a little bit more.

Backstage he can hear the pounding crescendo as the noise rises from a few clapping hands to thousands and then there are tramping feet. He's done this hundreds of times before and he knows just when the din can get no louder.

He slaps the drummer on the shoulder and nods his head. This is the third guy to sit behind the drums in the last five years. He's good, a pro as good as money can buy. He isn't impressed by celebrity but he's treated well, there are lots of girls at every stop and his cheque is large and dependable.

The drummer sprints in from the side, sits up behind his kit and brings both sticks down hard on the toms. The beating, chanting and whistling come to a halt and a roar rises from the cavernous room. He gives the crowd five seconds to cheer and steps out, tapping his chest and waving to the faithful. The building erupts.

This is what he's been waiting for. When he started, it was all about music. There was magic in the way that the four of them could combine their hearts, their hands and their souls to bring about the unity of a song. Somehow they transcended ego and played together in a timeless bliss.

But that was a long time ago. The bass player is the only one left from the original group and he's become sullen over the last few years. The new guys at least pretend they are thrilled to be playing, but the bassman spends much of the shows facing away from the crowd. He spends all of his time with his back to centre stage.

The thrill now comes from the adoration that flows in over him from these thousands of people. He can feel that they love him and he knows that many of the young girls and not a few young guys would be only too happy to have that love made concrete.

He was twelve years old when he understood that music was to be the core of his life. He learned guitar and piano, and when he finally tried, found that he could sing any note he desired. He was an awkward teenager with no friends. His parents worried that he spent all of his time in his bedroom playing and singing.

The world hit him hard. He felt the beauty and pain of creation unfiltered. It gave him grist for the song-writing mill but the brilliance of it hurt him deeply. He started playing clubs before he was twenty. The older players introduced him to the liquids and powders that made life just a little easier to stand.

Now he has no one to come home to, really no place that means anything special. There once was a girl who moved him, but she has been gone now for many years. Once too often he came home wasted with lipstick smudges on his shirt.

Now he lives for this wash of adoration. They love him and they justify his life. Five thousand people want him and wish they could be him, and until the end of the encore he will be happy.

A LOOK INSIDE

I should have spent more time in the pool. My wetsuit still fits just fine, my goggles aren't leaking and the water feels perfect, but it's obvious I'm outclassed here. My perception of the world is so muted. Something's missing from sound, sight, touch, taste and every other feeling I've ever had.

Reach forward and try to keep that arm up high, pull back in the water. Tip my whole body to the side and gulp in a little air as my face comes above the surface. Reach forward with the other arm, breath out. I'm sure I shouldn't be making so much noise; this isn't normal breathing. Don't panic, you can swim this distance.

Here's another pull and it's time to get a bit more air in. Shit, I'm not far enough above the surface and there is water in my mouth. I've got to be careful not to swallow or get anything down into my lungs.

Face back under the surface, now spit the water out. This is a little tricky, got to get air in and water out at the same time. This is making everything a whole lot harder. That cycle went by fast but now I need even more air than before.

This is supposed to be routine. I should be able to relax and concentrate on my stroke. That's the only way that I'm going to work up any speed.

Time to find out where I am. It takes a little extra work to lift my head up and I'm surprised how fogged my goggles are. This will have to do. I don't really need to see that much.

The first buoy is just ahead. It's a huge yellow inflatable monstrosity that no one could miss. It marks about a third of the distance I'll have to swim. Whenever I've done this course, I get a huge boost in confidence there. I look up on the next stroke and I can see that there are swimmers already past the second buoy.

Each time I've been in this race, I'm surprised by how far behind I get. You would think I'd get used to this. I'm certainly not getting any faster and there's no reason to think that the other competitors are getting slower.

I take a tight turn around the buoy and notice that there is another swimmer behind me and one just in front of me. There doesn't seem to be anyone else within twenty or thirty metres of the three of us. Incompetence loves company. I look again and the guy beside me is mocking me with some kind of side stroke. My front crawl must be pretty inefficient to keep me behind him.

We plow through the water together and settle into a clear hierarchy. The side-stroker is relentlessly pulling away and at the second buoy I make out the swimmer behind me gasping and grasping onto the inflated plastic. Looks like I won't be the last one out of the water today.

Time seems to dilate over the final stretch. I try to pull harder and kick with more fervour, but every time I look to the side, the scenery is unchanged.

Finally, I can see the bottom and all my worries of being pulled out of the water by a support boat or even drowning fade away. When I can touch down, I crawl along the bottom, pulling myself up to the beach. It's disconcerting to feel that I can move faster this

way than when I'm really swimming.

The run across the grass feels good. I'm looking forward to getting on the bike and away from my deficiencies in the water. The best triathletes can strip off their wetsuits while they run to the bike and then leap into biking shoes already attached to the pedals.

Pyrotechnical moves like that are beyond me. I'm not too proud to sit on the grass and haul off the neoprene and shove on my shoes, helmet and glasses. While I'm dressing, I notice two women pulling off their wetsuits and drying themselves at a leisurely pace. They don't seem to remember that this is a race and I feel no shame from passing them while they're changing.

It's a short run out to the road and I'm pleased at how efficiently I climb over the bike and clip into the pedals. There is a short flat section and then a little hill to climb. One of the joys of cycling is getting the gear shifts down to a place where you keep accelerating with the same cadence of your legs.

I feel like I'm flying up the first hill and I remember why I practice as hard as I do to compete in these races. The second hill is just a little tougher and I know that by the time I get to the top, my speed will be suffering.

The next section is a gradual downhill and I have to decide how hard I'll work. I want to take advantage of this gravitational assist, but there is still a lot of pedalling ahead.

Hills fly by and I've passed three cyclists by the time I'm into the town. There is a long slope through the business section that's a joy to ride through in a race. I often pedal through here, but the traffic is usually heavy and it's rare that I can really take advantage of this well-paved slope.

I don't have a speedometer on the bike for the race, but I think that I get up to around sixty kilometres an hour through the middle of town. That doesn't sound too fast until you've done it on a bicycle.

The course meanders through town and then heads back along the highway to the pond we just got out of. This is a long steep ride that I have ambivalent feelings about. I often ride this for practice, and I get the feeling that cycling uphill may be my one real strength. Every time I race this section, I pass other bikers. That feels great, but the cramps that almost always come at the top are excruciating.

Right on schedule, my left calf seizes up just after I've passed a seventh bike. The discomfort makes me slow down enough that one of them gets by me. I pound hard on the left pedal and some of the pain settles down. I'm able to push, but I have a feeling that my legs are just about ready to go off again.

I get past the pond without incident and I'm buoyed by my friends cheering me along. By the time I'm approaching the town again, my legs feel like they are ready for some more serious pushing. I'm not sure how they will react when I ask them to run, but that's a problem for later on.

I pass two more bicycles coming down the first section of the downhill through town. My bike is running smoothly and I'm going faster and faster down the hill. As the slope starts to flatten out, I start thinking about the run. I'm always amazed how hard it is to convince my legs to move after I've been on a bicycle. Perhaps my running shoes are jealous of the speed my cycling shoes get up to.

The bike is just up to top speed when I notice a white car pulled up perpendicular to the road. There is a woman behind the wheel and I'm certain that she makes eye contact.

I'm about ten metres from her when the car pulls out directly in front of me. At this distance and speed there is very little time to react, but I understand there are only two options. If I just pull on the brakes, I will certainly hit the car. The other possibility is to turn hard and brake at the same time. Either way I'm going down and this is going to hurt.

I jam both brakes as hard as I can and turn left. The bike responds in the only way it can and slides out from under me. Time is slow and I can feel the edges of my tires rippling over the pavement. My body follows and from the feet up parts of me contact the road surface.

The car drives away and two race officials come over to check on me. I don't think I lose consciousness, but the ambulance is here in no time.

For some reason it's important for me to prove that my head hasn't been damaged. I tell the attendants that my back is alright but I'm certain I've broken my clavicle. I've done this before on a bicycle and I'm getting to be a bit of an expert on this injury.

They ask me questions to assess my consciousness and I think I do pretty well. Of course, the person least able to evaluate a head injury is the owner of that head.

This is the first time I've been in an ambulance. I often look at these vehicles racing along the highway and cringe at the thought of the pain that the passengers may be in. I'm not doing that badly. Perhaps it has something to do with what they've run into my arm.

At the hospital, it turns out that my diagnosis was correct. I have an x-ray and the distal part of my collar bone is smashed to bits. The doctor says I need to sit quietly for a month or so to see if the bone will heal. At my age and with the seriousness of the fracture, it is possible that I'll need surgery.

I ask to see the radiograph and the image is disturbing. The end of the bone is in the wrong spot and there are pale splinters all over the place. None of this tells me much new, I can feel the shards of bone through my skin.

Two months go by and the bone heals well enough that I don't need surgery. My quiet lying and sitting around has allowed the bone to come together, but I'm in terrible condition. I'd always taken a shy pride in the muscle tone of my arms, but now there is nothing but bone and flab.

It's another month before I can start running again. It feels good to be on the road and doing something. The movement of my arms actually makes my shoulder feel better. Everything is progressing well until the morning I wake up unable to get out of bed.

There is a dull pain down my right leg, and I can't stand putting any pressure on that side. When I lift myself out of bed, the agony is so severe that I have to throw myself back down onto the mattress.

Something serious has gone wrong and I'm sure it relates to my spill off the bike. I go through sequentially stronger painkillers, but nothing can bring me to a state where I can comfortably stand.

The pain goes on for three days before I decide that I need proper medical attention. Even with the help of the numbing chemicals I've been consuming, it is impossible for me to get into a car and drive to the hospital. My wife convinces me that it is important enough to get help that we need to call an ambulance.

Getting on the stretcher and into the ambulance only hurts my pride. Arriving this way does have its perks though. I'm immediately looked at by a doctor and hustled off to the CT scan room. I've never seen one of these machines before. It has a science-fictiony feel, all cold and impersonal with odd metallic insect noises coming from it.

I don't mind going into the tube. I'm too concerned with what may be found on the scan. The doctors and attendants talk about how they are sure it will only be a disc problem. I came in here worried about my discs and it turns out that this might be the best explanation. No one mentions the word cancer, but it's obvious that's what everyone is concerned about.

When the scan has been analyzed and the results returned to the doctor, he comes in to see me resting as comfortably as I can on a stiff hospital bed. He's obviously not happy with what he has seen, and he wants another scan with contrast media.

I'm rolled back into the CT room and a nurse explains that she will be putting something into my vein that will make me feel cold. I don't feel the needle puncture my arm and the chill that comes on is of no concern to me.

A half hour later the doctor comes back and tells me that the problem is definitely with a disc in my back. Apparently, the disc between two of my back bones has squashed out its central jelly-like material and that stuff is pushing on a nerve and filling the canal that the spinal cord runs through. This is a lot better than cancer, but it's serious enough that he's made an appointment for me to see a neurosurgeon in a few days.

I'm not happy that back surgery seems to be in my future, but I'm relieved that there is a solution to my problem. Unless something goes terribly wrong, I'll be walking, running and cycling again before long.

The doctor has been reading from a sheet of paper that the radiologist has sent to him. I'm curious about the details of my injury so I ask if he minds if I read the report.

He hesitates for a few seconds and then suggests that while there won't be anything else useful for me to read, I can see the paper if I like.

I take the report and start into it. The part about my back is filled with medical jargon. There are lines like "hyperdense soft tissue nodular density in the right posterior thecal sac markedly indenting the right aspect of the thecal sac." Still I get the gist of what is being said. There is really no more information than what my doctor has explained.

There is another section in the report just after the part about my back problem. This takes up a number of paragraphs and I'm stunned to discover how much is wrong with me.

"Alignment is satisfactory. There are no significant bony lesions beyond degenerative changes to facet joints. Bilateral simple renal cysts and multiple bilateral parapelvic renal cysts. Mild atherosclerotic lesions noted on one arterial section. No areas of omental nodularity are identified."

I'm relieved that I don't have any omental nodularity, whatever that is, but I'm disappointed about the cysts, atherosclerosis, and degenerative changes. All along I had thought that I was pretty healthy. Sounds like there is lots going wrong inside me.

The real shame of all of this is that most of the information I've gained from reading the report isn't of any use. I spoke with my doctor and he insisted that every one of the findings outside of my primary problems are normal for someone my age.

I can see the fractured collarbone and messed up disc as some kind of battle scars. Being able to get a bicycle up to sixty kilometres an hour at my age is something to take pride in. And I feel entitled to a perverse vanity about this damage. Most people my age don't and can't put themselves in a place to sustain injuries of this sort. I feel that I've earned them.

But the cysts and the bony lesions and the atherosclerosis are wounds of a different kind. Everyone gets these. All you have to do is stay alive for a half century or more and you'll have them. I suppose they are earned as well. They are gained from the day to day pounding of normal life. I'm just not sure I needed to see them.

THE BABY

"It was so nice of you to invite us over for tea. Today has really been our first chance to visit. Alana and Tom are tired from their flight and she hasn't been feeling too well. We've just been taking things easy for their first few days here."

"I'll bet you and Tom are happy to be home with your Mom and Dad! Where you live so far away you don't get that many chances to get together as a family."

"Oh, we're both so happy to have them home. It was really a bit of a surprise. They are so busy with their work."

"I wish my daughter would find the time to visit me. Since she got her job in the city, I don't get that much chance to see her. I wouldn't mind so much except that now I don't get to see little Emily as much as I'd like. I could just eat that little darling."

"Any news about when they might be coming?"

"I went up to visit them when the little one was born. That's nearly a year ago now and I'm hoping that they will be back home again before too long."

"It's such a treat to see your kids, isn't it?"

"Mine hasn't been home for nearly two years now, but what I'm really looking forward to is a visit from little Emily. I'm certainly ready for them. Since Earl left me, I'm all alone here and the house can feel pretty big. No one ever stays in the second bedroom and I have it all set up for my darling granddaughter."

"Would you mind showing us the room? I'd love to see what you have done."

"Come on upstairs. I have all kinds of cool things to show you."

"Let's go up, Alana, and see what she's done in the room."

"That's OK, Mom, you two go on and I'll just finish my tea down here by myself."

"Suit yourself. Lead the way, missus, let's see what you have done."

"These stairs seem to be getting steeper every time I come up. Here's the room. Just down from me. When they come to visit, she can go off to see friends and party all she likes. The little darling will be fine just down the hall from my room."

"Wow! You've done a lot of work here!"

"If you are going to have a baby staying with you, you need a proper baby's room. Of course, the wallpaper is pink, that's what you want to have for a little girl. There is a crib that I picked up at Walmart when they had a sale. The old one we have in the basement isn't good enough anymore. You know they have all kinds of safety rules that weren't around when we had our kids."

"But we never had any problems. Surely your old crib would be good enough for a few days."

"You can't be too careful nowadays. The cribs that we had didn't have the special catches on the side that keep the gates from pinching the baby's fingers."

"I can't say I remember hearing about any baby's fingers getting caught."

"Well, that's just the way things are these days. Nothing but the best for my darling granddaughter."

"Where will your daughter and her husband stay if they come?"

"First of all, I doubt very much if that freeloader will be visiting here soon. I gave him a piece of my mind

when I was at their place just after Emily's birth. He doesn't do a thing around the house and I let him know what I thought. We didn't part on the best of terms. As far as my daughter goes, she can stay on a couch down in the living room. There's lots of room there."

"This place is sure full of toys."

"Emily loves stuffed toys. She's going to adore this big bear, have you ever seen anything so sweet?"

"That is one big bear. It's a good thing you have it here. I'm not sure how you would ever get it on a plane to get it to her place."

"Oh, no, you don't understand. This is Emily's bear and her mother will be taking it home on the plane whether she likes it or not. That bear was expensive and it's not staying here taking up room in my house. Now I don't care so much about the rest of these stuffed toys. They can leave some of them here if they like. But I'm expecting that they will want to take most of them."

"That sure is a lot of toys."

"But look at how sweet they are. See this bear with the cute little tie and the tiger? Couldn't you just take him home with you?"

"They are lovely, it just seems to me there's an awful lot of them."

"Here now, look at this lion, what a cutie. Why don't I take it downstairs and give this one to Alana? No doubt she'll be having a little one before too long. This would be just great for her baby when it comes. How old is Alana now anyway?"

"She's thirty-five and has been married for ten years now."

"Well they certainly are taking their time with the kids. You must be buggin' her all the time to get on with getting you some grandchildren."

"It would be nice to have some grandkids, but we don't talk about that much. We figure that's their business."

"I'll tell you I wouldn't be quiet if I had to wait that long. My daughter isn't even married yet. I'm expecting they will tie the knot to make things easier for Emily. Most of the young people don't seem too concerned about those kinds of things these days. But I'll tell you, if she had been married, I would have let her know I expected some little ones."

"We should get downstairs again. The room is lovely, but poor Alana is down there by herself and our tea will be getting cold."

"Hi again. Alana, your mother and I were upstairs looking at the baby's room. I'm all ready for Emily to visit. You would have loved the room. I've got the place packed with toys for the baby and I was telling your mother that you are welcome to have a stuffed toy if you'd like one."

"That's very nice of you, but we are really limited in what we can take back on the plane. We try to travel with just carry on, so there isn't much extra room. I enjoyed the tea, but Mom and I should get back to the house."

"Now just wait a minute. I haven't even shown you any of the pictures or videos that I have of little Emily. Here are some pictures of her from when I visited last year. Now she was just a newborn in these, so she doesn't look much like that now. But look at how sweet she was. Look at those little toes and fingers."

"They are lovely, but we should get going."

"Here now, here are some videos that I have of her. We talk on Facetime and I record our little chats. Look, look at what a sweetheart she is. See how she looks up at me. I can tell that she knows who her grannie is. Here. Look at this one, she's crying here, doesn't want to be in front of the camera, she must be tired. Isn't she sweet?"

"The videos are really nice, but we need to get home. I'm not feeling so good. I think I'm not over the jet lag yet. Mom, I need to get home and get in bed for a while."

"I'm sorry, sweetheart, I didn't realize that you weren't feeling well. We had better be going. I'll be down again to see more of your videos of Emily. You certainly have a beautiful granddaughter. Thanks for the tea."

"Well thanks for coming over. It was so nice to see you, Alana. It's been a long time since you've been around. I remember you so well as a little girl. We were all excited the day your Mom and Dad picked you up. They were so proud. That was a special time in this corner of town."

***

"Mom, thanks for getting us out of there, I'm not sure I could have stood another minute. I know she has good intentions but that visit just about drove me crazy."

"Ah, sweetie. I'm sorry to have put you through that. I wouldn't have taken you over if I knew you would be upset."

"The whole visit was baby this and Emily that. She doesn't realize that everyone doesn't get excited about the idea of babies. It's fine if you have your own, but for some of us, things aren't that easy."

"Do you want to talk about this, or would you like me to leave you alone?"

"Mom, Tom and I have been married for ten years now and we have wanted a family even longer than that. We have tried and I hope that you're not disappointed that you don't have any grandchildren."

"Listen. We have never pressured you to have kids and it doesn't make any difference to us whether you don't want kids or if you are having trouble having them. We are happy with you and we think you have a wonderful husband. That's all that matters to us."

"But I feel like I've let everyone down. We have had all kinds of tests and there don't seem to be any problems with Tom. This whole mess is because of something wrong with me. All my friends are having kids and that's all they can talk about. I get so sick of the whole thing. There are even times when I've thought of doing away with myself. I'm that disgusted."

"Now hold on just a minute. Do you think that your ability to have kids has anything to do with your value as a person? You are just fine the way you are, and no one is suggesting that there is anything wrong with you."

"But Mom, I've always wanted a baby. You know what I was like when I was small. I always liked dolls and I always pretended they were my kids and now in the real world, none of that works."

"Sure, that's a disappointment. But there are other ways around things and there are other important parts to life. It's none of my business, but have you and Tom ever thought about adopting?"

"We talked about it for a while. But that whole idea seems like an admission of failure to me. Surely an important part of our life here on earth is to pass along something of ourselves. In some way we live on through the parts of us that go into our kids."

"But don't you think a part of you could go on through children that weren't biologically your own? Doesn't loving them and bringing them up make them a part of you?"

"That's easy for you to say. This stuff is just all theoretical for you. You have no idea what those possibilities really mean."

"OK. This isn't going to be easy. One of the hardest things a parent ever has to deal with is the question of how much to tell their kids and when to tell them. When we were down the road visiting do you remember our neighbour's parting words?"

"No. It was probably something about how wonderful Emily is."

"That's not right. Don't you remember her talking about how proud your Dad and I were when we went to get you? When she said those words I just about jumped out of my skin. I looked at you and wondered if you would catch on to what she was saying. I'm sure if you were paying any attention to her at all, you assumed that she was talking about us bringing you home from the hospital. We didn't go to a hospital to get you. I'm sorry it's taken so long to tell you. But we have more in common than you have ever dreamed and we're doing just fine."

WHERE IS YOUR STING?

Today is Pattie Northcott's twentieth birthday. Her mother took her to the finest restaurant in town for a wonderful meal. The freshly baked bread, the squash soup, the stuffed chicken and the cheesecake were delightful.

It's raining again on her birthday, but she is happy in the quiet of her bedroom. Her cat Beatrice doesn't move as she runs her hand along the animal's back. It's been a perfect day. Pattie covers herself with a down comforter, lies on her back and peacefully folds her arms across her chest.

Pattie's father was very sick when she was born. She doesn't have any memories of him standing. He was always in bed, confused and coughing. Her mother understood the trauma of growing up with a sick father who was in constant agony and tried to compensate by ensuring that there was no pain in young Pattie's existence.

As her father grew more and more uncomfortable with life, her mother started enthusing about the peace that he would sometime gain. Every day she reminded her daughter that someday soon his suffering would be over, and he would move on to a better place.

Paul Northcott did indeed die just before Pattie's fourth birthday. Her mother made a brave attempt to picture his death as a time of joy. In the funeral home Pattie saw her father lying peacefully and for the first time she could remember he had the suggestion of a smile on his face. He wore a neat suit and rested comfortably on lavish silk. She could see the reason her mother had insisted this was a positive occasion.

From the day of the funeral, Pattie's mother redoubled her efforts to keep discomfort from her child's life. To ensure that Pattie wouldn't see the horrors of real life, there was no television in the Northcott home. Pattie was homeschooled for the elementary years and her mother carefully redacted the uncomfortable sections from her world history texts.

Pattie grew to be a happy, if somewhat restrained, child. She saw the world as a benign place that rewarded good deeds fairly. Her mother gradually invited young neighbours into the house and Pattie developed rudimentary social skills.

When she reached high school age, her mother decided that she was well-equipped enough to venture out into the real world for a few hours each day. She drove Pattie to school every morning and picked her up as soon as the bell rang.

Although Pattie had acquaintances at school, it would be an exaggeration to call them friends. She gravitated to the goth kids. Their outlook on life seemed reasonable to her even if she disliked the music they listened to.

Halloween was her favourite night of the year. Her mother was relieved that there was one evening she looked forward to going out of the house. At the same time she was concerned with the pleasure that her daughter took in devising ghoulish costumes.

In grade ten, Pattie was given a school project to write about ancient Egypt. She was a serious girl and read what she could find on the internet. Egypt turned out to be much more exciting than she had ever imagined. The three-thousand-year span of the civilization dwarfed everything about our current culture. The Egyptians held their world together with advances in government and agriculture. The pyramids hint at technologies we still don't understand. But with all this wonderment, what fascinated Pattie most was their ideas about death.

She found the concept of mummification fascinating. The removal of brains through the nose and the thirty-day process of preparation excited her in a way that nothing had done before. She read and reread the descriptions of organ removal, salting of the body and the final stuffing with sand and linen.

It was during her second-last year of high school that Pattie decided that she would apply to mortuary school after graduation.

There was a thin boy with thick glasses in her class whose father ran the funeral home twenty minutes from her place. She began eating lunch with him just so she could ask questions about the funeral business. Of course, he mistook her interest in the profession for something else. Soon she was volunteering every weekend at the parlour.

The boy's father took to her immediately. It wasn't often that he met someone who showed such sincere interest in his work. He explained to Pattie that the funeral business really wasn't about dead people. It was about those left behind. He went so far as suggesting that a funeral for someone with no friends or relatives left really wasn't a funeral.

The director recognized Pattie's sincere desire to become a mortician and he took her under his wing as an apprentice. When a grieving family came in, Pattie would watch this meticulous man navigate the fine line between compassion and business. He would listen attentively to whitewashed histories of the deceased and tactfully introduce the realities of casket selection and burial details. Pattie understood the skill shown but could never find the patience or interest to talk to living relatives.

Her true passion lay in the preparation of the dead for disposal. She was disappointed when immediate cremation was chosen. The bodies would be refrigerated until the time of burning. It was when cremation was delayed or even better, when the body was to be buried, that the real art of the mortician came into play.

She came to love the smell of formaldehyde. The draining of blood and replacement with fluids somehow moved her. The dead came in through the back doors of the funeral parlour waiting for mortuary magic to shift them from grey wraiths to radiant objects of splendour.

Pattie had not used much makeup before she started her time at the funeral parlour but she came to understand how cosmetics could change a body completely. She never considered it a compliment when a mourner would say that Pattie's work had made the dearly departed almost look like they were alive. She always thought her job was to make them look better than life. She removed cares and frowns that were a real part of living people and she gave them a peace they may have never known.

Mortuary school took two years. Pattie learned a little more, but most of what she needed she had already seen in her work at the funeral home.

The lectures on ethics and morality left her uninspired. Surely, she thought, her work as a mortician was to serve the dead. Corpses had no cares about how the relatives were spoken to or how much they were charged for services. Pattie saw that her clients would be at a vulnerable place in their lives, but she never really understood why this should be.

The science she was taught at school was marginally more interesting. Pathology and microbiology left her cold. These were the domain of the living. Her real clients had no pathology or microbiology that made any difference. Anatomy was a little better. The structures of the body were still with the dead and knowing the layout of a corpse helped in transforming it into a thing of beauty.

Her real interest in school was in the practical sessions. She couldn't get enough of the talks on embalming and the restorative arts. This was to her where the real work and value of her profession lay.

Pattie graduated in the middle of her class. Her instructors marvelled at how someone could show such brilliance in parts of the curriculum and absolute lack of interest in others. She never made any friends at school. Her classmates seemed to be divided into those whose parents ran a funeral home and confused middle-aged loners looking for a change of career. None of them changed their natures enough to bond with the others at school.

Pattie has been at work now for a full year. The funeral director understands that it's best to keep her in the basement. She's an artist with the clients and everyone in town knows that their establishment puts out the most pleasing of corpses. In the last six months, no one has said the departed look just like when they were alive. This is partly because of the fuss Pattie made when one charming older lady commented on how lifelike of her departed husband was. The town knows about the incident, but that isn't the only reason no one says Pattie's work looks lifelike. There is something about her bodies that makes everyone smile and then wonder why they did.

The director's son has a girlfriend now and she doesn't work at the home. The son is easing his way into his father's place. He finished mortuary school two years before Pattie and he understands his mission in life. His calm and caring demeanour and careful suggestions for services and amenities comfort grieving families.

Pattie knows she will never be a director and she is thankful. On the evening of her twentieth birthday she calmly drifts off to sleep wondering if she should have used green irises for the eyes in Beatrice.

A Thing of Beauty

Since arrival, her parents shared an unwavering certainty that she was the finest looking child to have ever been born. I would urge great caution in putting much credence in this opinion, as it is common for the newly-hatched to be greeted with assertions of this sort. There are children with swollen heads, asymmetrical eyes and twisted noses who receive the title of most beautiful on first appearance. We must be careful trusting mothers and fathers in the matter of the beauty of their newborns.

All of this aside, she was quite a normal-looking child. She had the proper number of limbs and her eyes, nose, and mouth were all in places that most people would agree to be appropriate.

For the first decade of her life, the question of her attractiveness didn't take up much of her attention. Her parents and relatives continually reminded her that she was one of the great beauties to have ever inhabited the earth. Because she was told this so many times, she unthinkingly accepted the conclusion.

There was an occasional little boy who would tell her she was ugly, but she had learned from a very young age that little boys were strange and defective creatures. She had no brothers and her father acted nothing like the young males she encountered outside the security of her home.

The first chinks in her armour of self-acceptance came just before she entered the teenage years. At a birthday party for her thirteen-year-old next door neighbour, one of the presents was a glossy fashion magazine. The girls huddled around this portal into the fantasies of post-adolescence and rhapsodized over how they would one day look just like the models in the photographs.

That night, for the first time in her life, the girl carefully examined herself in the full-length mirror in her mother's bedroom. She realized with a shock that she looked nothing like any of the women in the magazine.

Not only were these creatures taller than her – she had always understood that adults towered over children – but everything about them was different. Their faces looked as if they had been covered over by a smooth and shiny coating of paint. Nothing like the blemishes on her own cheeks were evident on any of the paper women.

Their hair was longer and thicker and fell just so across their eyes and ears. She realized her own hair was a dung-coloured mess that drooped unpredictably in unappealing tangles.

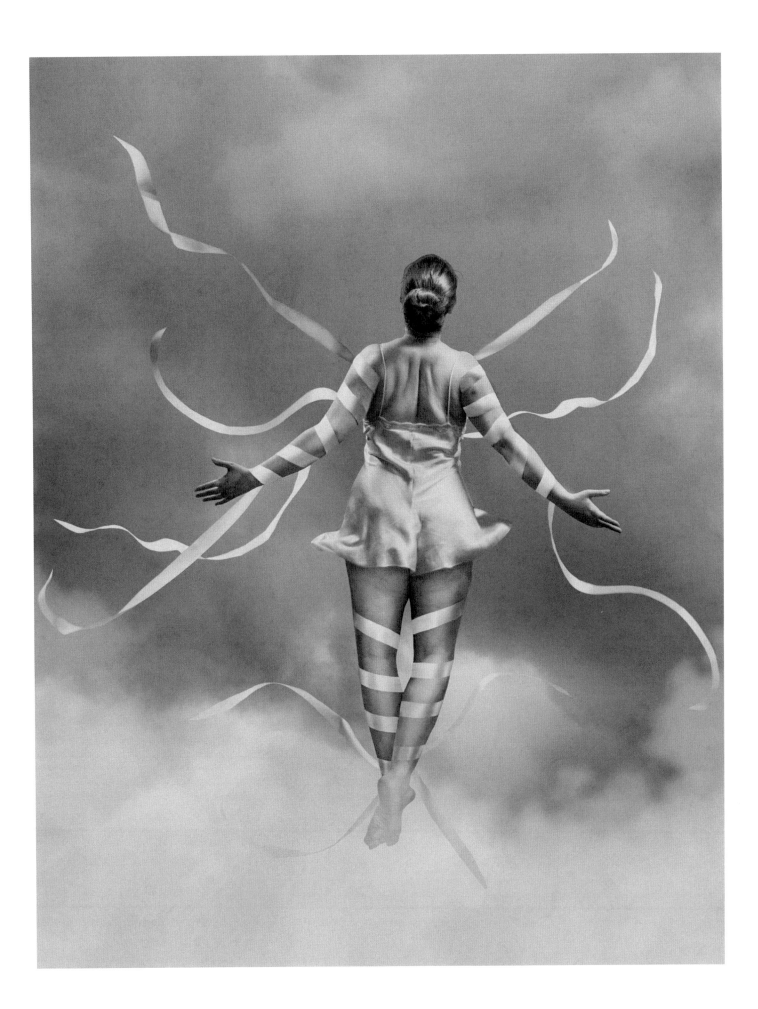

Perhaps the most disturbing difference was the shape of these women's bodies. Every one of them looked strong, but not strong like her athletic friends at school. These people had robust shoulders that sloped away to a trim waist and then ample hips. Their chests looked like nothing she had seen at school or even from her mother's friends.

That night she went to sleep with dreams of beautiful women and a slight hope that sometime in the future she would develop into one of these human swans.

The next day of school wasn't helpful. She had never noticed before how different she looked from all her classmates. Some had smooth long hair that floated when they turned their heads. There were a few with brightly-coloured lips and shaded eyelids. The popular girls were tall and slim. Even the heavier girls who stayed to themselves had curves she didn't possess.

Her attempts that night to convince her mother she needed makeup were unsuccessful. She told of her impressions of the models in the magazine and explained how some of her friends looked more like these women when they coloured their lips and put on eyeshadow.

Her mother laughed and suggested that these people were freaks. Normal women didn't look that way and the pictures weren't even accurate representations of what the models really were. The editors of the magazine spent hours changing the photographs to hide any suggestions of imperfection.

She went to bed disappointed in how little her mother understood true beauty. It was becoming clear that her family had always lied to her about her appearance. Obviously she was plain if not a little ugly and no one close to her had the decency to admit this terrifying fact.

The next morning, she set about developing a plan to recover her lost sense of beauty. She began with an assumption that beauty and attractiveness were essentially the same. In order for a person to be beautiful, she by definition would have to attract the attention of others.

The girl started into a rigorous survey of her classmates to find what it was that made some of them more appealing. After a full week of careful observation, she came to the conclusion that there were two factors that were involved. Girls that spoke well and those that excelled in athletics were the most popular.

On reflection, this was not an encouraging start to her quest for beauty. She knew that she was too shy to ever be appreciated for her conversational skills and she had almost no interest in sports.

It was time for a serious re-invention. She first tried to insert herself into discussions amongst the most popular cliques in school. Invariably her efforts at conversation were met with long silent stares. No words were needed to let her know she wasn't welcome in those elevated circles.

Her attempts at talking with the less tolerable girls went a little better, but she soon understood that she wasn't looking for the acceptance of this class of people. No amount of practice with the lower classes would ever elevate her eloquence to the level she required.

As much as she disliked sports, it became apparent that this was the only realistic path to beauty. She started hanging out in the gym just watching the other girls to see if she could understand the appeal of all that work. The room itself was an odd place. It smelled of something old and threatening, and the echoes of the bouncing balls and screeching sneakers suggested an empty loneliness.

A gangly blonde shooting baskets struck up a conversation and invited her to try. Her first attempts were pathetic, but the blonde was kind and encouraging. Before long she could throw an occasional ball through the hoop and felt a moderate sensation of accomplishment.

The girl suggested that if she kept at this and started running to get in shape, she could make the school team.

This was the first indication that there was some path to her goal and she even ran a short distance on her way home from school that day. Over the next few months, she spent more and more time on the basketball court and increased her running until she could go for a full hour without stopping.

The girl's basketball coach noticed her rapidly improving skills and soon she was a part of the school team. Unfortunately, the year was nearly over and she spent most of her time on the bench.

This lack of playing time didn't discourage her. She realized that she had put her toe over the threshold of one of the temples of beauty and attractiveness. She ran hard all summer and spent hours on outdoor courts.

When September came around, she easily made the starting lineup of the school team. Her skills continued to improve with coaching and she became one of the top players. Despite the team's success in tournaments, she always understood that all of this activity was only a means to an end.

By the time she was in high school, she was one of the best players in her city. She was popular with her teammates, but none of the other girls or any of the boys paid her any attention.

The day after her team won the city championship, she went home alone to contemplate what had gone wrong. She looked at herself again in the mirror and realized that she had made a serious mistake in her earlier calculations.

Beauty and attractiveness, it turned out, weren't quite the same thing. A person could be attractive because of attributes other than beauty and she had no interest in that kind of appeal. She remembered the women in the magazine and the true beauty that shone through them.

The girl she saw in the mirror was no closer to the models than she had been when she first encountered the magazine. Her hair was cut short for athletic efficiency and made no concession to style. Her legs were massive from her continuous exercise and she had no curves anywhere.

That was the last day she played basketball.

With careful consideration she came to the conclusion that makeup and diet were more effective routes to beauty than exercise. Her mother could no longer stop her from properly fixing her face. She spent most of her allowance on cosmetics and scoured books and videos on how to properly prepare herself.

The process was more difficult than she ever imagined. Every time she worked at her face the results were either unnoticeable or clownish. Many of her sessions in front of the mirror ended in tearful breakdowns.

She eventually came to a compromise that, if somewhat garish, did conform to the standards that most of her friends attained.

Her first attempts at dieting were unsuccessful. She began by having no breakfast and a small lunch, but soon found that this only resulted in her binging on supper and snacks in the evening.

She began to record her weight every day and was soon disgusted by the wild fluctuations in her mass.

In her last year of high school, a new girl in the area began talking with anyone who would listen about the cruelty of eating animals. She found herself cornered by the proselytizing newcomer and offered a defence that anything that tasted as good as bacon couldn't be wrong to eat.

48

The new girl was horrified by the suggestion and started into a long description of the cuteness and intelligence of pigs. Her eyes were just about rolling up in her head when the activist added that a vegetarian diet was also one of the best ways to lose weight.

Now she had her attention. The animal lover in front of her certainly was slim and if there was a simple route to weight loss she was interested.

Just a month of a strict vegetarian diet brought results. Her weight dropped and she soon found herself not missing meat. She never did worry about the treatment of animals. Her vegetarianism, like basketball before it, was for a specific and narrow-minded purpose.

Her eating habits soon evolved to a strict vegan style and her weight continued to drop.

She visited the mirror more frequently and developed a certainty that the closest predictor of beauty was weight. She came to a firm certainty that it was impossible to be too slim.

Research brought her to the conclusion that the most beautiful people in the world were the contemplative Buddhist monks of southeastern Asia. Her thinking led her to an understanding that beauty had nothing to do with the thoughts of others. The acceptance of peers or strangers and even the classic ideas of beauty from the long forgotten fashion magazine were trips down the wrong trail.

After high school, she spent a year in university studying philosophy and losing weight. Nothing in her classes changed her ideas about the importance of beauty or her conclusions about its nature. Her positions became so solidified that a year of education was all she could stomach. So much of what her teachers suggested conflicted with her own beliefs that going to lectures became painful.

Out of school, she embarked on a pilgrimage to Asia to find the source of all that is beautiful. She wandered through Myanmar, Cambodia, Laos, and finally ended up in India.

The beautiful white bearded, wild haired, and emaciated mystics from the mountains seemed to her the epitome of what she was searching for in life. It disappointed her that none of these holy men would teach her or consent to having her live with them. They all insisted that part of perfection was being alone.

She found herself in an ashram that catered to tourists and spent hours in meditation and discussion with the monks. Most of their talk was bland nonsense scripted to draw money from the pockets of wealthy visitors.

One day, as she sat meditating in the garden, a visitor from England engaged her in conversation. While she normally shunned the company of anyone from outside of India, this man told of his own search that in many ways mirrored her own.

He wasn't interested in appearance, but he had come to a decision that the way to truth was by giving up on attachment. His conclusion was that only by turning your back on everything in the material world could you find enlightenment. The part of his story that appealed to her most was his idea that eventually even food could be forgone.

He said he had heard of a mystic in the mountains who had completely stopped eating and existed entirely on air. The only problem the man had was that he was in constant danger of floating away and had to tie himself to a rock.

The next morning she gathered up a coil of rope and began climbing.

The Final Act

I have always thought that helping others is an important part of life. In order to find meaning, it's critical that we think about something other than ourselves. I suppose that's why I have been a member of so many volunteer organizations. And I guess that's why I'm at this interminable meeting this weekend.

The room is stifling, but I have to admit that the lunch they provided was good. Interesting sandwiches, a lovely red pepper soup, crisp salad, and a nice selection of bars and pastries for dessert. As always, it was a bit of a trick eating all the stuff I picked up without making a mess of my pants, shirt, and notes. They really should have some better plan than bringing the food to our meeting tables.

I know I ate too much, I've never been good at passing by the attractive things in life. You'd think I would have learned that food can't be judged by its appearance. Nothing can.

Now I can hardly stay awake. The facilitator they brought in drones on in front of poorly-designed slides. It took her twenty minutes this morning to get the projector hooked up to her laptop. Can't blame her for that though. I don't think I've ever seen a presentation where the tech worked properly.

She's supposed to be guiding us towards the construction of a vision statement and saying things about silos, spitballing and skill ecosystems. Actually she doesn't say these things, she "speaks to them".

I joined this organization because I wanted to help others. Now I find myself with a group of people spending the money we have put so much effort into raising on some clown telling us that the most important thing we can do is to put into words what we are doing.

The money spent on renting this room, paying this facilitator, and providing that fabulous lunch would have been better put towards our real purpose.

I don't have the nerve to say these things out loud. I've been reminded too many times that I'm not much of a team player.

So I sit back, try to keep my eyes open, and think about so many things beyond this ridiculous mission statement.

We have a break and Tom comes over for conversation.

He rolls his eyes conspiratorially and comments on how fascinating the day has been.

I laugh and suggest that the red pepper soup was almost good enough to make the trip into the city worthwhile.

Tom wonders out loud how much the organization has paid the facilitator and leans in as he concludes that this whole weekend has been a waste of time and money.

I have my own reasons for being here and I can't say I'd really rather be anywhere else, but I don't share that thought with Tom.

We met three years ago when I first started working with the organization and soon recognized each other as pragmatists. I'm not sure there are too many more like us in the room. Maybe though, we have been guilty of silence. If we had expressed our concerns about the way things work, there may have been others finding the courage to speak out. I have to be careful here or I'm going to use the word "silo."

Tom asks how Louise is doing.

That one sort of knocks my breath away and I'm surprised and disappointed how long it takes me to answer.

I give a noncommittal response and steer him back to the quality of the lunch. I'm actually relieved when the facilitator taps a spoon on her glass and asks us all to take our seats so we can get going again.

The rest of the afternoon drags along painfully, but I don't feel any relief when she passes out the predictable evaluation sheets. She may think that the cute cartoon at the top of the page will soften any criticism, but she doesn't need to worry - I'm not in the mood to be complaining about anyone.

I fill mine in with mid-level ratings for a low-level performance. As much as I hate standing around talking about last night's game and tomorrow's weather, I join into the nearest small circle I can find and nod and smile at the inanities being served.

I'm the last guy out of the room. The facilitator was gone as soon as the evaluation sheets were handed in. She's as mercenary about this as she could be. I know she was well paid and couldn't care less about the work of our group. I hope that I'm not becoming too cynical as I age. There are so much more important things to get worked up about than this meeting.

I take the stairs instead of the elevator and spend some time looking at the photographs in the lobby of the hotel. There is something about the one of the rocks in a misty lake that looks more like a painting than a photo.

If there wasn't a piece of glass in front of the work, I'd run my fingers over the surface to test its authenticity. Appearances can be deceiving. You never know what it is you are looking at and you don't know what it is that people want you to think you are seeing.

I realize that I'm delaying the inevitable and I force myself to walk out into the parking lot and start up the car. It's tempting to stop off somewhere for something to eat, but I know it's time to go home. Louise will be waiting.

The drive takes about forty-five minutes, but in my mind it could have been anywhere from ten seconds to a week. There seems to be some kind of temporal vacuum between the hotel and my house.

I pull up in the driveway and grab my overnight bag from the passenger seat. My hand shakes a little as I unlock the front door and I call out that I'm home. You never know who could be listening.

I walk down our short hall and into the dining room and see Louise sitting at the table. There is a bottle of rum and a half-filled glass in front of her.

"So you changed your mind. For all your insistence, I wondered if I might find you sitting up just like this."

I move around to her side and soon realize that she isn't moving. Her head is upright and she isn't even slouched in the chair, but she's gone.

This isn't the way it was supposed to work. She was to be in bed. But this will do, there are just a few things that I need to take care of.

I touch her on the shoulder and tell her that I'll be right back. Up in the bathroom, I make sure that all of the pill bottles are hidden away. They are empty so there is nothing to flush down the toilet. For some reason, I take a cloth and some Windex and wipe down the vanity top and mirror. Something drives me to do a quick polish of the doorknob. I think I watch too much TV.

Everything looks to be in place. There's nothing suspicious about this scene. Louise has been going downhill with her cancer for years now. The last few months have been especially brutal. I can't complain about her drinking. I'm not sure I would have behaved any differently if I were going through the pain she's suffered.

Just moving air in and out of her lungs was an effort for the last few weeks and I can understand why the plan made sense to her. She suffered through the hollow optimism of her family doctor and she was adamant that she would never have anything to do with physician-assisted death.

She hated that term. "Call it what it is, it's suicide. Have the decency to be honest about it. What difference does it make if a doctor or a partner or a friend helps you out. This one's on me, it'll be my decision."

The love had gone out of our relationship a long time ago. She knew about Karen and even commented that another woman would make me happy when she was gone. I know I was never much of a husband, but I also realize she didn't wish me a life of misery alone.

She was decent in the end even though she must have realized the guilt this would bring on. I don't think that was ever her intent. I know I always overthink these things.

I call Karen and tell her it's done. When she offers to come over, I insist that as much as I need her now, it will look very bad for her to be here.

I call 911 and report the death of my wife. The scene has been sanitized as well I can manage and I sit down at the other end of the table.

I thought there would be a lot to say, but all I can do is stare at her across the reflecting hardwood.

Lovers who come apart are more common than the ones who stay together. Before we married we both had a burning desire to be as close to each other as we could. We thrilled to breathe each other's breath and touch and touch and touch. The trajectory of desire was like a sine wave. It fell as quickly as it rose.

We found ourselves comfortably indifferent. That would have been enough for me, but when she lost her job and started drinking and smoking even the affection dried up.

The men and women I know are different species. Girls become women long before boys become men. But I think they pay for that early start. Even when Louise and I lost interest in each other, I still longed for the touch of someone. She didn't care.

An ambulance drives up our street with its siren wailing and stops beside my car. I wonder what the hurry is. There's nothing these guys can do that has any urgency.

A muscular young man with heavy black army boots and wraparound sunglasses knocks heavily on the door. The girl behind him has her hair tied back severely and stands with her legs shoulder-width apart and her hands on her hips. I get the impression they would like it if I didn't answer so they could kick in the door.

There are terse introductions all round and they spend a long time feeling for a pulse on Louise. It's important to me that I don't say anything. I can only make things worse.

Before they've given their expert opinion that the patient may be dead - they remind me that only a licensed doctor can make this definitive diagnosis – two police cars have pulled up outside.

The officers are all men and three of them spend their time talking with the female paramedic. The fourth policeman warns the guy in the sunglasses not to move anything in an obvious attempt to assert his dominance.

He tells me that he will have to call the coroner in before we can move the body and he would like to go somewhere private in the house to ask a few questions.

We move out to the kitchen and he begins a rigorous grilling. I try to explain quickly how sick my wife has been and how much trouble she has had breathing. Throughout the interrogation I'm careful not to say anything that could be construed as an opinion.

I won't say that I'm not surprised she has passed on, or that I've been worried about her depressed state. I try to play the part of a shocked and saddened husband.

When he asks about her psychological condition, I'm especially cautious. I don't want any suggestion that I might have foreseen an overdose of pills. Now that the coroner is getting into this, I'm worried that they'll cut her open and see what's inside.

There's really no reason to think that I would have anything to do with an overdose, but you can't be too careful.

The other three cops have pried themselves away from the ponytailed girl and are starting a thorough search of the house. I wonder if they think they'll find a meth lab in the basement. The two paramedics make themselves comfortable on the living room couch and find my stash of National Geographics.

The questioning goes on and on, but I think I'm doing a reasonable job of saying nothing. It seems my interrogator has just about run out of steam when one of the other officers comes in with a birthday card from Karen that was on my bedroom dresser.

He asks what the card is about and I explain that it's from one of my friends at work. I hope he isn't so thorough that he checks up on this.

The cops say they don't have any more questions at this time and wonder if I mind if they look around the house a little more. This must be a rhetorical question from a bunch of guys who have already been through my bedroom. Still I nod wordlessly.

I move out to the living room with the paramedics and bury myself into a magazine that I've read every word of. I've got through an article about Vikings in Scotland and a disgusting one on the number of mites that share our lives when the coroner arrives.

The man looks like he's slept in his shirt and starts off complaining that this is the fifth call he's had today. The cop who questioned me brings him over and introduces us. The coroner offers quick condolences and says he's got a murder that he needs to attend as soon as he's finished here. His apologies for putting me through an examination are more to himself than to me.

He walks around the table once and doesn't touch Louise. I give him a terse medical history and he responds that it's pretty obvious that this is a heart attack. He signs a sheet for the paramedics and leaves. It's amazing what power and knowledge a medical degree can confer.

Everyone else leaves the house at once satisfied and disappointed that nothing out of the way has occurred.

I immediately phone my friend from darts who works at the funeral home. I say that Louise has passed on and I would like her cremated as soon as possible. She has no family beyond me and I'm not interested in a funeral. I don't explain that I'm also in a hurry to get rid of this last piece of evidence in my house.

We talk for a while and he eventually admits that the minimal service is to remove her in a cardboard coffin and cremate her without embalming. When I press a little, he says it's possible to do all of this today.

He arrives at the house within an hour and his assistant helps stuff Louise into the cardboard box. She's a little stiff and doesn't lie out completely flat.

With a little manipulation they manage to get the lid closed and just before they leave, they ask if I'd like a moment alone with the deceased.

The only reason I agree is that I worry that it would look suspicious to refuse. They tactfully step outside and stand in that funeral worker way of stiff uprightness and folded gloved hands.

I pull open the cover and the light coming in through the window in our front door catches her eye. There is a momentary flash from her cornea and she says thank you.

I tell her she's welcome.

Arachnoid

She sits at her desk and picks up a book. Its empty pages are bound in leather. She felt that this lavish piece of stationary would instigate creativity. But she sits and nothing comes.

She remembers reading about the difference between real life and story. It would be pointless to write about the real world as it slowly ambles by. Most of life is meaningless. To write, one must capture those rare moments of significance and wrestle them onto a page. A story needs something beyond the meaningless and mundane.

Perhaps, she thinks, there is nothing in her life worth writing about. In order to create anything worth reading, she may need to go outside of herself. Pure invention might do it. She wishes she had a life more like her heroes. If she were an athlete or a singer, her existence might be worthy of ink.

She puts her book down and looks around her room. This place is a metaphor for her whole being. It's an ordinary – no, a boring place.

Her bed is unexceptional. There isn't even a headboard. The sheets are an off-white cotton with pills from too many washings. She knows that her pillowcase hides a bag of duck feathers stained yellow from tears and drool. In her sleep she's even more pathetic than when she's awake. That pillow must be crawling with mites and bacteria. There's a miniature world making its home under her head. She needs a new pillow before the thing smothers her some night.

It might have been her grandmother who made the quilt. There is no rhythm that she can discern to the pattern of the patches. The randomness of the colour makes her think of Mondrian. But it's Mondrian with more nerve of palette.

Her house is old and the floors are fashioned from planks put there over a hundred years ago. She can make out grooves that have been worn through the years as successive inhabitants made their way in and out of the door. The planks are wide, wider than any trees that grow within a hundred miles of her home. This wood may have come across the ocean centuries ago. She can see that the two knots closest to her desk resemble the eyes of a cat. They slant in an appropriate fashion, and in each one she can make out an iris and a pupil.

This room was covered in linoleum when her family moved here. The wood looks so much better. She can remember how much work it was to take off the old floor covering and how disappointed they all were when they found the floorboards covered with a dirty white paint. They tried toxic-smelling paint removers and scrapers before they decided to rent an industrial sander. The gouge beside her chair bears mute testimony to the madness of that machine taking on a life of its own.

There is a window just beside her desk, but she keeps the curtains pulled because she knows that the view outside would only distract her from her writing. The wind is blowing hard and she can hear a branch scritching across the clapboard. Some people can write with music on, but she prefers sterile silence. Sometimes she wonders whether she should get a set of the industrial yellow plastic ear protection headphones she has seen on carpenters.

Two walls of her room are taken up with books. It would be so much easier to read than to write. The world of her childhood sits there, lined up so much neater than her life. Escaping to Narnia or Hogwarts always made life more bearable. The temptation sits there today. It would be so easy to pull down a book, preferably some-

thing simple, something she's already read.

She resists and looks back at her blank page. Still nothing. Her eyes wander to the bookshelf to her left and then up to the corner of the room. There's a spiderweb there. Nothing too impressive - she's amazed it could have sprung up so soon after she tidied the room. Cleaning is always such a virtuous excuse for not doing what she knows she should.

She has four eyes that bring in a kaleidoscopic vision of a large mammal below her. The animal doesn't move and she knows it's far too big to kill and eat. If it dies by itself, she could get nutrition from the decaying flesh and that might give her the energy to raise another batch of offspring.

Time doesn't matter. The future will come and the past is gone. But she remembers that she had young once before. The male found her from the pheromones she left on the web. He mated her and sealed her up with his webbing so no other male could claim her. It didn't matter to her. She had no preference between the males she'd seen. He was the first to come along and he was all she needed to give birth to others. He was quick about it and scurried off when the job was done. She knew she could have injected him with a little venom and eaten him, but there had been enough flies that she was full when he visited.

There were hundreds or maybe even thousands of eggs and she had no idea how many of the brood survived or where any of them were now. They were capable of looking after themselves as soon as they swarmed out of the eggs and she wouldn't tolerate anyone competing for the insects in her part of the world.

There was nothing in the web this morning. It's time to eat the webbing and start into another trap. She knows every section of the web and in what order she will have to consume the lines to keep the structure from falling to the floor.

Eating the web doesn't give her pleasure, but something inside her makes her understand that she needs nutrition to keep on existing. The web is old now, its stickiness is fading and the insects in the area may have learned to avoid its specific location.

She's been sitting here without moving all night. Now it's time to begin. She doesn't move like the mammals. Their muscles are fine for nutrition when they rot, but what an inefficient way to reposition extremities. She's all heart. That organ drives her blue blood through her body and by shifting it hydraulically, she can cause her legs to move. She can jump so much farther and faster than the mammals, even faster than the stupid insects.

Now the old web is gone, but before she starts another, she'll take one trip down to the floor to check out the environment. She starts with just a little silk from her spinneret and tacks it tight to the ceiling. This first bit of material is sticky, but for the rope she'll use to drop herself down, she'll make a thicker strand with no adhesive properties.

The spider watches the mammal as she silently abseils down through the room. These huge creatures are strange. They are dangerous. She's had trouble with this one destroying her webs, but when she lowers herself in close to the beast, it screams and runs from the room. How odd. The creature is large enough to crush her with ease and she knows her venom wouldn't be enough to stop it. Still it fears her.

At the floor, she cuts her rope and with just a little stick, fastens it so that she can use it to return to the ceiling. She knows that she could climb the wall, but it's so much faster going up a web strand.

She scuttles across the floor and over the canyons in the wood. When she stops, she watches and listens for other beings in the room. Her sight is exceptional and she's sensitive to vibrations from any size of animal moving through her environment. After careful scrutiny and analysis, she's confident that she and the large mammal are alone. This will work well. She's a little disappointed that there are no insects around. But they will come and if they aren't here while she spins her web, they'll be less likely to know it exists.

She climbs back up the rope and eats the webbing as she ascends. The protein is too valuable to waste.

If she were outside, it would be easier to build a web. In that world there is always the movement of air. When she hangs from a section of web out there, she can always count on the wind to shift her so that she can start her first line.

It's a little more complicated in here. She attaches a line a little way from the top corner of the room and then walks to the other wall, letting out web as she goes. When she reaches the other side, it's a simple matter of pulling a little in and then attaching the end to the wall. She has one strand that's tight and well positioned. Now it's time to put that beautiful design in her head to use.

This pattern is deep inside of her. She walks along the main strut with another gossamer line trailing from her spinneret and then moves a short distance away from the end to fashion a V. Now she has a frame to set her orb on. It's not hard to measure out the distance between the waves of web. At each intersection she makes sure the strands connect and before long her masterpiece is done. Throughout construction she takes care to only touch the ends of her legs to the web. It requires considerable attention to not be caught in her own trap.

The geometry is perfect and she's laid down sections that are sticky and smooth in the right combinations. From the edge she plucks a strand and listens to the tone that confirms the structure's tension is perfect.

Today's web is finished and after one walk across it, she'll rest on the edge and wait for the day's nutrition to show up. With most of her legs folded under her and three of them wrapped around a line of the web, she feels invisible to the world.

The large mammal hasn't done much. She wonders where it gets its nutrition. The thing sits here most days but doesn't seem to accomplish anything. Insects have come by and it hasn't even noticed. She supposes she should be grateful that it isn't competing with her for food.

A foolish fruit fly comes into the room. These insects are so stupid. With their wings and antennae, they feel superior, but they never even sense her trap. The mammal doesn't notice as the fly comes in close by her head. No doubt the insect is attracted to the smell of the monster. She just doesn't get it. This fly only feeds on rotting vegetables, but still she has to check out the mammal. Doesn't she know that this monster can reach out and crush her? And it's violence for no reason. She almost feels sorry for the insects she has seen obliterated by the mammals. These beasts seem to kill for fun. She's never seen one consume a single victim.

The fly has had enough of the mammal and she's headed right for the web. Come on darling, just a little further into the corner. She knows that she has the best sight of anything in the room. The extra eyes don't hurt, but it's really about the attention that she puts into things. She may look like she's just resting up against the wall, but she's watching and feeling everything that happens in this fascinating room.

She sees the fly hit at the same time as she senses the vibration of her web. Even in full darkness when her sight is limited she would have known she had a visitor to her lair. Now is the time for patience. The thought of that beautiful fly starts the juices of venom going, but she'll wait and make sure it's well bound in her net before she comes out for a visit.

It's not long before it's obvious this fruit fly is going nowhere except into her gullet. She strides out along a cord and injects it with just enough venom. That will stop all of the irritating squirming and soon the insect will be liquefied enough for her to take in. Why would she bother with jaws and teeth when she has such an exquisite feeding system?

The fly will do her for another light cycle. Perhaps she'll leave the web up for another day. It's still early and she has enough nutrition to last her over the darkness. There's a good chance another insect will come into the web and she'll have some rest while she watches over her cached food.

This is a fabulous location. The temperature is constant and there are no strong winds to destroy her creations. She hasn't seen a male here for quite some time, but that hasn't been a priority since her first brood. She's found an excellent place to put her web. She hasn't moved it since she came here and every time it goes up, it provides insects. Who could ask for a better place to live?

She looks up from her empty page and sees a little spider wrapping netting around a fly that's almost too small to see. She thinks about what pathetic and repetitive lives these puny bugs live and closes her eyes hoping that something inside of her will provide a story.

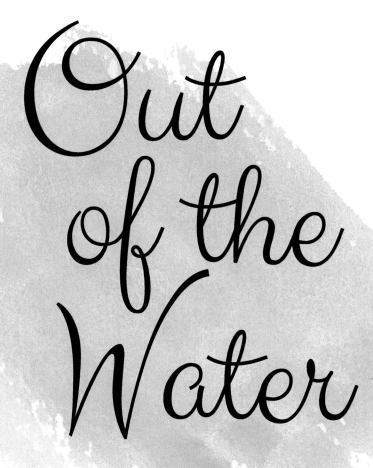

Out of the Water

Thanks for havin' me in here, man. It's dry in here out of the water. Look at that shark comin' up to the window, black and white, black and white just like a shark rollin' up, two sets of eyes staring out the window. They're always movin', you know it's like they can't breathe unless they move? They're lookin' for me, man, don't look at them. It'll just get their attention and they'll come in and tell both of us to move along. It's good though that there's a crowd here, they won't hit us.

These fries are great, I love this place, warm, good food. Not like out there in the water. Too many people though, too many people in tight, makes me think all kinds of things with all these people around. Sometimes I think things I shouldn't think, man. They think I don't see them, but I do, I do. Out there in the water, I watch them. They walk up to me and they walk right by me just like I'm not even there. I watch them walk by and look away. They can't see it, but I've got them all figured out.

Look at that guy up at the counter. Big chain hanging out of his pockets, useless sunglasses tipped up on top of his head, legs spread wide like he owns the world. Hands on the counter, chattin' up that cute little girl with the braids. Look, look she was talkin' to him and he just cut her right off and started talking on his

phone. He's real loud, seems like he wants everyone in here to know he's on the phone. That's his type, man, he thinks he's a big shot, he wants everyone to think he's important. But he's not, look when he leans forward, the bottoms of his shoes, the soles man, they're just about worn right through. He's all looks man, all looks, there's nothing to him inside. He's hollow, man, he's hollow.

Now he moves away and that girl with the braids, she's laughin' at him. She'll do that all day, man, she smiles and tips her head down and looks up through those long lashes at the guys and they think they've really made an impression on her and then they leave a little change when they walk away. And when they walk away, man, she just scoops up the change and laughs at them, she laughs at them all. Sometimes she tells the other girls behind the counter something and they all laugh, I can see her game.

Look at the guy with the mop. Looks like a loser, bad face, teeth crooked, thick glasses. He just smiles to himself while he cleans the floor. Seems he's got something funny he's smiling about, but nobody else can see it. And that girl with the braids at the counter, she smiles at him a different way, she just looks up quick and looks away when he looks over her way. She's different with him, man. She has it figured out, he's nothing special, but he's the real deal, man. Nothin' put on with him, man, he's just what he is.

And those three, look at them. They're real quiet, just a word now and then, they're watchin' everyone. Man, they just looked over at us. What do you think they're up to? Look at all the frizzy red hair on that one, look at all the books they're carrying. Man, they're eating fries with cheese and gravy, that's poutine, you know that stuff? Poo teen. Funny name, eh? Funny though none of the teens are eatin' it even with that name poo teen. Ha ha, pretty funny eh?

Hey, look out the window, there's the shark again - a homodont, I remember that from school, they're all the same. He's huntin' now, he's on the move, lights flashin', siren blastin', I wonder who he's after. He's not after me, I'm in here. It's dry in here, no sharks, that's great, man. Whoa, he's gone, he's gone, that's good we can relax.

And look at the kids in here, man, they're just like shadows. I try to do that, but I can't do it like them. You sit here and a couple of them just float by. Just like shadows, unhappy shadows though man, there's something wrong there, man. Look at all the makeup on those girls, they put it on like housepaint, what a mess, look at the tight pants, man, somebody must have painted them on too. No way that's really them inside those shirts, man. And that scrawny kid, man, with the fluffy top lip, what is he three feet tall? What, maybe what, 80 pounds? Lookit him, comes up to that little girl and he's huggin' her, man, huggin' her. Look man, both of them look away, there's nothin' there, they can't even look at each other. Now, now, now, another of those little girls comes up and hugs her too. They both gotta do it, man, can't get left out. Did you hear her, man? "I love you." I love you, then she looks down. She doesn't know what love is, man, nobody at home loves that kid.

Man, I used to know what love is. Man, somebody kicked it out of me and I can't find it any more. Somebody kicked a lot out of me. Just like the song, man, I get a kick out of you. Who did that song, man? I don't know, maybe ABBA. That's from the Bible, man, it's ABBA, it's a message being sent to us. ABBA, that means father, did you know that? One of those guys in ABBA he had a kid with one of those girls, he's the father, man. He's ABBA, do you think that's right?

But, but, maybe that's wrong maybe it's got to do with four, there's four in the band and ABBA, that's four letters. Man, that's an important number, man, four, the four horsemen of the apocalypse. Apocalypse, man, that must come from ca- lypso, you know that music from down south where it's hot? You could say hot as hell, excuse my language, sorry about the language, you think that's all a coinci- dence? I don't think so. Listen to ABBA, man, they're trying to tell us something, man.

What are you writing? How come you're writing down so much now, man? It was great you brought me in here and got me the fries, man. I really appreciate this, man, in out of the water, away from the sharks. Even if we didn't get the poo teen, man. I'm not sayin' you should have got me poo teen, but it does look good, man. What are you writin' there anyway? What you doin', man, you writin' some kind of story about me or something?

Hey, I got an idea for your story, man, how about you drive up in a fancy car just for a snack? You're not even hungry, just for a snack and you find me out there huddled up against that dumpster and its pourin' out, man, it's pourin' and you bring me in here for some fries. No, how 'bout poutine? No, no, wait, that wouldn't work, nobody would believe that, just have yourself get me some fries.

BOOTS

Get comfortable, this could be a long one.

Stop me if you've heard it before. It's a story from back when I used to do a little more nutmeg than I do now. Not that I ever used that much; a little pumpkin pie here and there, some raw spice rubbed on the mucus membranes now and again. Really nothing serious, never put the stuff right into the lymphatics or anything.

So, my daughter Toad - funny name Toad though, it came from the gardening accident that we don't talk about anymore. Toad asks me to tell her a bedtime story. Dad, Dad tell me about Puss 'n Boots.

Now, I never heard of this Puss and Boots, but I don't really want to admit this deficit in my literary education to my little girl. From the way she enunciates the title, I just know this is some classic that I missed in my misspent early days.

The first thing that comes to mind is that it must be some tale about a cat in a boot. Maybe this is a story about someone who gets sick of old Puss and cranks her down into a piece of rubber footwear and sends her off for an outing to the bottom of the nearest amply-depthed body of water. I'm just opening my mouth to relate this when it occurs to me that it isn't the sort of dissertation that poor Toady would appreciate just before bedtime.

I close my mouth long enough to think up a coherent story that will do as a substitute nightcap. I'm pretty sure boots doesn't refer to footwear, it's more likely another character from the story. That's it, Puss and Boots. Chances are Boots is a dog.

So, there were these two friends, Puss the cat and Boots the dog. They lived in a big house on a small field and they had very little to worry about. The only terror in their lives was the mouse that lived in a hole in the wall of the hall just before the bathroom door. The mouse, who Puss and Boots didn't know the name of, made itself at home every night when the humans went to bed. And every night that mouse ate just a little very old cheese. As a result of this that rodent had the worst breath that anyone could imagine. Just a cough from a foot away would melt candles.

After its nightly nip of cheese, this mouse - whose name I don't know any better than Puss or Boots did - would bring its family of even smaller mice out onto the living room floor and tell stories with an accompaniment of rancid halitosis.

Puss and Boots would cower by the front door.

On the evening in question, this mouse started into an ant story.

In a field very far from here there was an ant called Marvin. Marvin was a special ant. He had travelled far and wide and he knew tales from many places. This ant had another special feature. Ants as you know, have eight legs and Marvin only had six.

Do you know what ants eat? Not many people or mice do. Ants are so small that we don't pay much attention to them. They're turophiles. A big word that's really kind of useless because there is an easier way to say it. Ants are cheese lovers.

Now you're thinking, aha, this has something to do with the mice. We all know that mice are turophiles and it was mentioned earlier in the story that the unnamed mouse was particularly interested in aged varieties of cheese.

But stories don't always work that way. The cheese infatuation of ants has nothing to do with the mice in the story. I'm not even sure why I bothered to bring up the relationship between ants and cheese. As a matter of fact, I'm not even sure that it's true. But let's get on with the story.

I mentioned before that Marvin had done a lot of travelling. Now, he's never been to Ouagadougou or navigated the Limpopo River, but you have to remember that he's just an ant. Unless he got onto a boat or an airplane by mistake he wouldn't have a chance of doing the kind of exotic moving around that you would expect from a person who claimed to be well-travelled.

Marvin had been all around the field that he lived in and had spent considerable time in the house that sat on the hill that bordered the northwest side of the field. While in the house, Marvin would slip into the cheese cupboard. I know that most people around here keep their cheese in the fridge, but that's really not necessary. In countries where cheese is most valued, you could even say in turophilic countries, cheese is almost never kept in the fridge.

While he munched away in the cheese cupboard, Marvin would listen to the people in the house. His memory was good and when he returned to the anthill, Marvin was a big hit telling stories from his cheese-centred excursions.

After a particularly fruitful visit to the house, Marvin called all his ant friends around to tell the story of his latest travel. He articulated clear, linear, sensible stories, so there was always a big crowd of ants for Marvin's talks.

He climbed up on a small rock, looked around at the gathered ants and rubbed his front two feet across his mandibles.

"Just yesterday I made another expedition to the big house where the people live. After I finished up in the cheese cupboard – last night it was an exquisite old cheddar - I saw the small girl walking to the room she sleeps in. Feeling brave and full of cheese, I followed. A man came in and sat on the edge of her sleeping platform. The girl asked him to tell a story about the dog and cat that live in the house. It wasn't much of a story, not clear and sensible like the ones I tell, but it does feature cheese rather prominently - and this is how it goes…"

Reveal

    I can't really say that I know much about him, either before I started this story or since, but to her, he seemed like a nice boy. After they met at a physics lab in school, they went for a walk that stretched out over two hours. He listened to her with an intensity that she had never felt before. In her experience, boys didn't behave that way. They stared and made sick jokes, but this guy seemed different.

    She had never understood the appeal of boys, but deep inside, she realized that girls didn't interest her much either. People her age were shallow. Her best friend had been fun until this last year. They had ridden their bikes together and explored secret paths through the woods near their homes. But now her friend was interested in a boy. She found this incredibly boring.

Now, it may be helpful at this point to provide a little information about the girl. She is seventeen years old and I think it would be fair to call her attractive. Not beautiful to the point where modeling agency scouts would be banging at her mother's door with multimillion-dollar contracts in their sweating palms, but certainly pleasant in appearance. Her mouth and eyes were symmetrical and she did smile most of the time. It is interesting how often beauty is less about what you have than how you use it. A person with a classically beautiful face and body can completely ruin the impression with a bored or sullen disposition. But I digress.

When her friend first found this boyfriend of hers, they still spent time together. But more and more of her conversation centered on the boy. It didn't take long before all of her time was spent with him. Her friend was gone, but a part of her wondered how much she had really lost.

I hope you were able to follow that last paragraph. It sometimes gets confusing when a story is told using the impersonal she or he rather than given names. I can see how you might be confused about who was actually talking with the boy and who was losing who as a friend. I could go back through it all, but I'm just going to give you credit for figuring out the characters and their activities. Perhaps we should move on to the real action of this story.

It was only a few days after she met the boy in question that she asked him if he would like to go camping. He appeared to be astounded at her suggestion, but quickly recovered his composure and was soon as excited as a puppy.

It may seem unfathomable or even inconceivable (although I'm not sure that is the right word) that a young girl would invite a boy she has no burning interest in for unaccompanied time together in the woods. I'll just have to ask that you either believe that there are girls who would behave this way or just suspend your disbelief long enough to enjoy the story.

They set a time two weeks ahead and she was surprised to find herself excitedly counting off the days to the trip. See, she's not quite as unusual as you may have thought. She had gone camping many times before with her family and with her best friend, but there was something different about this trip that she couldn't quite put her finger on.

One of the changes was that this boy had a car. When she had camped with her friend they always just walked into the woods near their houses. On the more exciting trips they had rides from their parents. It was great to get farther from home and into the woods, but depending on others for a ride had always taken some of the adventure out of their trips.

The day finally came and he pulled up to her residence in his car. Things got off to a poor start when he tried to take her packsack and then opened the door for her to get in.

"Do you think I'm some kind of weakling? I can lift my own bag and open doors for myself."

The boy looked down at his shoes and quietly apologized. The girl wondered if she had perhaps been too harsh.

It surprised her that they didn't talk all the way to their destination. This was a new friend and she worried that she had ruined everything by complaining about his groveling. He was a boy after all and he didn't understand how girls worked. At least he didn't understand how this girl worked.

She knew most of the girls at school loved it when the boys lifted things for them or opened doors. They were a weak-minded bunch - silly girls who couldn't look after themselves.

I don't think it's too much of a stretch to think that a seventeen-year-old girl might think and act in this way. There are girls of that age who have become tediously uninteresting adults, but I've certainly run into some that are quite a bit like this character. Perhaps you were even a bit like this in your own youth.

They arrived at the parking spot just a little after noon and started off into the woods. He was a good walker. When she had hiked with her friend it was always frustrating how much she had to slow her pace and they often spent more time resting than she liked. With this guy it was different. He could walk as fast as her and she had to admit that he even pushed her a bit.

They had walked for nearly three hours when he asked if that was enough for the day. She was tired and her feet did hurt a little, but she had never admitted to anyone that she couldn't keep up.

"I'd be happy to walk some more if you're up to it."

He shrugged his shoulders. "Just thought you might like to stop. This isn't a bad place for a tent and I've had enough. But if you are keen, I'm happy to walk some more. Let's go."

She kicked herself for her quick answer, but couldn't see an easy way out of going on. They had gone about another half an hour when she tripped the first time. The boy had learned something from their discussion and didn't comment or offer to help her up. An hour later, she stumbled twice and the second time twisted her ankle. As hard as she tried, she couldn't keep from letting out a little yelp.

The boy turned to look at her, opened and then quickly closed his mouth. He sat on a stump for a while as he looked up into the darkening sky.

"You know, I've had enough walking for a day. How about if we stop here for the night?"

I have to say that this is quite a clever boy. I'm not sure I would have had the patience he's showing here. But I wonder if this may all be a show, perhaps he has a longer game plan than we're giving him credit for.

She smiled and agreed that this was a fine place to put a tent. She didn't even complain when he moved around behind her and lifted off her pack-sack.

She groaned quietly, rotated her shoulders and reached up to rub each side.

"I could rub your back a little if you like… no maybe that's not a good idea. We should set up the tent and get supper before it gets too dark."

He understood how to put up a tent. It was obvious that he had done this before, he knew just how the poles, fabric and pegs went together. The tent was assembled a lot faster than when she had gone camping with her friend.

Now, I can't really claim to know that much about tents, but they can be a real nuisance to put up. The few times I've been camping, I've needed the instructions to figure out how all the parts go together. Sounds like this guy knows his stuff, but I've never been all that impressed with people who make things I find difficult, look easy.

They hadn't really talked about supper. She assumed that each of them would just bring a meal and eat their own food. He rummaged through his pack and pulled out a butane stove, some camping pots, and three plastic containers full of food.

"I made up some Indian stuff - there's some raita, a curry, and naan bread. Did the curry by myself, I cook a bit for a hobby. There's lots here for both of us."

She thought hard about the can of beans, two slices of bread, and apple that she had brought.

"Sure, sounds like a good idea. I won't bother taking out my food and we can split my apple for a dessert."

"An apple sure would go good after all that walking."

He lit the stove and heated up the curry as skillfully as he had put up the tent. Supper was delicious and she was exhausted by the time they cleaned up the dishes.

I have to say that this guy is getting on my nerves a bit. First, he can put up a tent with no effort and now he cooks Indian food for a hobby. He sounds too good to me. I'm starting to wonder if he's some kind of a serial killer or animal abuser.

The boy took out a lantern-like apparatus with a small candle inside and soon had the tent filled with a gentle light. They blew up the mattresses and put their sleeping bags next to each other.

She didn't understand what came over her, but the words were out of her mouth before she could stuff them back in.

"Would you still be interested in rubbing my back?"

Her shoulders were aching, but she wasn't sure why she would want some boy to have his hands on her like that.

"Just lie down on your stomach and I'll fix all the knots from our hike."

Right, he's going to fix the knots from the hike. I can see where this is going. I had hoped to put together a meaningful story, but this is turning out to be just a tawdry bodice ripper of a yarn.

The boy was just as skillful at massage as he was at the niceties of camping. He pushed and prodded into tired muscles in a way that hurt just enough to feel good. The best was when he reached down along the sides of her neck to squeeze the tops of her shoulders.

"You're sure you don't mind this?"

"Mind it? That feels so good."

See, I told you so. This is not going to end well.

With that the boy reached under the bottom of her shirt and ran his hands along the sides of her spine. She felt herself swimming away through a happiness that she had never felt, as if something in her had let go or moved away.

"You know if you undid that strap back there you could really get at my back."

There was no hesitation from the boy and soon he was massaging from her shoulders to her waist.

Her whole body felt warm and the tightness from the day melted away. This was nothing like camping with her friend and this was nothing like the security that she felt from her parents. Maybe this was why her friend had moved on to boys.

She realized that she had never revealed who she really was to anyone in her life. This boy seemed special and perhaps it was time to expose her heart.

"Just stop for a minute. I'm going to roll over."

And that's it? So what happens next? Does he chop her up with an axe in the night or does she strangle him? Frankly, I thought I could have done better than this. Not much excitement in any of it. For all I know they could end up getting married, having kids and living out happy lives. And that wouldn't be much of a story.

I Found You

Aurora, I found you.

It's been nearly forty years, so perhaps I should tell you a little about where I've been. I married the girl I left you for. She's perfect. She had to be for me to leave you. We have three kids and they're all doing fine. The whole family is happy.

I think you know that I worked for the police department. It really was a steady job. There was adventure and I honestly believe I did some good. But you can only spend so many years tracking down missing kids and watching lawyers do their worst. And so I quit and started my second life as a writer.

It started out slowly, but I'm doing well now. There have been three bestsellers in the last seven years and the movie from the first book will be out very soon. Because of all the publicity around the movie I was certain you would hear my name and maybe read my books.

I've never forgotten you – loyal and beautiful with your astonishing eyes and long shining hair. You were my first love and the first person I ever shared my deepest thoughts with. We smiled and laughed and taught each other how special someone outside ourselves could be. Together we fumbled through the elementary mechanics of buttons and clasps and an introduction to anatomy.

Somehow we lost track of each other. After we both moved away, I kept in touch with some of our friends. None of them seemed to know where you had gone.

Every few years I made a half-hearted attempt to find you. Curious, with big parts of me worried about what we would do when we came together. This year I finally decided that enough of our lives had gone by that seeing you again might not be an intrusion. I spent considerable time on the internet searching for you. I started with your maiden name and then moved on to looking for your parents and sisters. With such an unusual last name I was sure it would be easy.

I thought everyone would leave a trail on the web. You don't need to do anything special to be on the internet – run a race or have your children in a music recital and your name will be in there. But for you, I found nothing.

Then I remembered the name of the guy you were going out with when we last spoke. It took a lot of searching before I found the picture of your grave. It was in an obscure French-language genealogy site under a section on your father-in-law's death.

Ten years.

You were gone ten years before I found you. I looked at that little picture of the burial plot of a man that lived five houses away from my family. I remember his wife with the black eyes and bruised forearms. My parents told us she must have been clumsy. There was a small flat stone in front of his that mentioned his son's wife had passed away at forty-eight years of age.

I kept closing the site and opening it again another day hoping that one time I wouldn't find your name and those years chiseled into that cold rock. I even tried to convince myself that the final date might mean the year your marriage ended.

I took to the internet again and I found your sister. Phoning her was as difficult as the first time I called you for a date.

She was kind on the phone when I asked if we could talk about you. But she floored me with her comment that your passing wasn't that much of a surprise. She said you had tried to take your life a number of times before. It was only after my reaction that she understood how little I knew.

I told you that I write now. Like all writers, down deep I write about myself. The connection may be hidden in caverns of words, but something of me leaks onto every page. Someone said writing is easy - all you have to do is open a vein and pour your life out on a sheet of paper. But that analogy seems so cheap, so cruel and inappropriate when I think of you opening real veins and pouring your life out into a bathtub.

I asked your sister if you ever pierced your ears. I knew you well enough to be sure you never did. You were always afraid of pain. What could have driven you to finish like that?

All I ever wanted Aurora, was for you to be happy. Was that too much to ask? I've been happy and you deserved it every bit as much as I.

Suicide. It's a word we all hide from. I can say it now. But it just doesn't work with "committed" any more. People commit a crime, they commit adultery or murder. You died by suicide, but there was no committing. I can remember years ago believing that suicide was a selfish thing to do. Now I understand differently - I see that it was selfish to think those things.

You knew what you wanted, you knew what you needed,

and you got it. Your life was a burning twentieth story apartment and your only option was to jump out the window.

You weren't well. The note you left doesn't sound like you. Your sickness was as tragic and physical as the worst kind of cancer and just as terminal. I can't say I'm happy with your choice, but you have passed through an opening to some place where you won't suffer any more.

I have no right to grieve you this deeply. I left you and I know it hurt. As irrational and wrong as my guilt is, it still aches.

I don't know what to believe about death anymore. It always seemed simple when there was no unfinished business with loved ones who died. But you are different. I wonder if you ever thought of me over the years. I'm sure you had no idea how often I thought of you. I wonder if there is still any you. Can you understand how much I miss you?

Aurora, I hope you can see through the thin layer of varnish over this story and know how much you are loved and remembered.

Brave

When I was five, I was brave.

The yard behind our house was a big one. There was lots of room to run and there was a slope that dropped down to our fence. The fence was to keep us in the yard. We understood that we were to stay inside and that danger lurked beyond.

One day when my brother was three, I took him through the gate behind our house.

The grass grew high, so high we could barely see. We went straight out from the fence and reached a trail. We walked for a long time and could hear the river running alongside us. The trail turned and came up to the edge of the river. The river was wide. I could see the other side but it was far away. There was a board across the river and I stood on the end of the board. The board swayed and I knew I could never cross without falling in. Just standing there almost made me sick. The fear ran through me so I turned with my brother and ran back along the trail. We could see our tracks through the high grass where we had come out from our yard. Our hearts were pounding when we came back in through the gate. I was brave.

When I was fifteen, I was brave.

Before that time I knew that girls were different. They were fun to tease, but mostly they were in the way and they didn't understand what fun was. One day I suddenly understood that girls were interesting.

There was a dance at school for Christmas. There would be a real band and the gym would be decorated. Some of my friends had gone to the dances before, but I never understood why. Cathy made me understand. She was the prettiest girl

I'd ever seen. With long brown silky hair, she had thick lenses in her glasses that gave her a mysterious air. I sat by the phone with pen and paper and wrote out clever lines. "Hi, I understand there's a dance at school next week. The band is supposed to be very good. Have you ever heard them?" No, wait, should I say my name? Perhaps I ought to talk about the weather first. I filled three pages, crumpled the paper, and made my way to the phone with a pounding heart. Turning the dial seven times with one finger made me sweat more than running five miles. Her mother answered and I slammed the phone down. Thirty minutes later I called again and Cathy answered – "Willyougotothedancewithme?" I was brave.

When I was thirty-five, I was brave.

My job required me to work with animals. The animals often didn't appreciate the help I tried to bring. I was bitten, scratched, cut, and kicked. There were times I was dealing with an animal that could easily hurt me and I didn't even think about the danger.

But other times, I would walk into a barn and look at a horse with a large cut on its side. The horse would be frightened by its wound and unhappy with the idea that anyone would come near it. The wild look in its eyes, the pulled-back ears and the thrashing legs made it an intimidating creature. I understood that the safest place around a dangerous animal was in very close. After a deep breath, I would dive in quickly and stand right next to a half-ton of furious beast. Getting there was only the start; once my breathing slowed there was the issue of driving a hypodermic needle into muscle, an action sure to prompt a wildly violent reaction. I was brave.

When I was fifty-five, I was brave.

Since I moved to the town I spent my career in, people knew me for what I did. My profession defined me; people knew me as the vet.

But there came a time when I decided that there were other things I wanted to do with my life. My job had entailed being available all day and night seven days a week. Activities like camping, fishing, and weekend excursions were difficult to plan. I wanted to write, to paint, and to travel. Quitting work meant I would stop doing what I had dreamed of since my youth and I'd no longer have the position I enjoyed so much. To retire meant to become the guy who used to be the vet. It is not an easy step, but I did it. I was brave.

When I was seventy-five, I was brave.

It wasn't until I was nearly sixty that I realized my life was more than half over. Still it wasn't until years later that I had the time to think of the consequences of this reality.

There came a point when life slowed down a little. My abilities decreased, but my aspirations stayed high. I wanted to do so many more things, but understood that my mind and my body were not as capable as they had been. The end seemed suddenly uncomfortably close, but I was not in any way ready for its cold embrace. While the thought of my mortality scared me, I looked it clearly in the face and continued to enjoy my life. I was brave.

Now I am ninety-five and if anyone ever happens to think about me, I'm sure they think I am brave.

I fear nothing. I know who I am, but I don't care if anyone sees or understands this.

Death is certainly near, but it holds no fear. My friends and my partner are gone, one of my children is gone. My time has come.

Perhaps the thing I miss the most is fear. Without it, it is impossible for me to be brave.

I am ninety-five and I am no longer brave.

It's so simple.

It's so messy.

It's so easy.

It's so hard.

It Comes Down Hard

This bus is cold. Everything about it - the thin seats, the metal walls – they all want to suck the warmth right out of me. The woman beside me hasn't said a word for the whole trip and despite the frigid window I find myself leaning away from her. The snow is coming down in fine arrows hurrying on their way to where we've just been. I can make them out clearly in the headlights of every car that comes towards us.

It's been a long trip and my feet are frozen. I wonder if there isn't some way they can heat the floor of this machine. My head is leaning on the backrest and I'm hypnotized by the white particles flying by. I have no idea how long I've been looking out this window. A frame of ice is slowly evolving around the glass and with the heat of my finger I can make the pattern just a little more interesting.

We never signed any papers and we didn't have kids, but we did have a house and we lived there together for four years. I always thought that house was our home and I always thought of her as my partner. Never did think of her as a wife, but don't get me wrong, she was a big part of my life.

It didn't bother me at first when the guy from her past phoned. They had been together for a short time back when she was in high school. I wasn't too pleased when she said he was coming to our town for business and wanted to meet us. Maybe I shouldn't have told her to go on alone. Maybe I should have come along for supper that night. But, hey, if she could leave me that easily, maybe we weren't meant to be together.

So I gave her the house. It turns out I gave them the house. He had one of those online jobs where he could work anywhere, so he decided he'd move in as soon as I moved out.

And here I am on this bus. It seems our friends were really her friends. There was no one left for me in our town. At first I moved into an apartment on the other side of the tracks, but my life in that place just seemed empty. My work was seasonal and I could do the same thing just about anywhere.

We all need a home. Not everyone has the luxury of having a home where his heart is. If your heart and your home don't fit into the same building, sometimes you just have to move to someplace new and hope your heart comes along for the ride.

I tried that, shifted on to the next town down the road, but it was empty. There were people there and work and places to stay, but I couldn't find anything powerful enough to keep me from moving on.

The bus is bringing me back to the place where my heart once was. I grew up in this town. Just saw a sign that said we've entered the municipality. Back when my heart was here, life was simple. There were four of us – Mom, Dad, and brother. I don't miss brother. He and I never saw eye to eye. He's a big shot now, a lawyer.

I'm not even sure if he's still in Vancouver – that's how much we have to do with each other.

But Mom and Dad were good to me. I suppose I wasn't as grateful as I could have been. The trouble with school and the trouble with the cops – they didn't ask for any of that. It's really just now sitting here in this machine that I can see it must have been rough for them.

When Dad died, Mom had some trouble finding me. That was before I moved in with her. Into a house that I don't even own a piece of anymore. Those were my wild days. After I shifted away, I was a classic no-fixed-address kind of guy. But Mom found me and she paid for the bus ride back to the funeral. I had a few drinks before the ceremony and there were some words between me and brother. It was easy for him with all his money to visit the old man and woman. I never had nothing.

That was probably seven years ago now and it was the last that I saw of any of them. But still, this town and that house are the only places I can think of that my heart belongs to in any way. I'm a different man now and I'm sure Mom will see it when I come in through the door.

It was late morning when I got on this bus and it's dark now. The snow looks different as we glide in through the town. The lighting's better and I can make out more of the world around me. Off the main highway and down the main street, the white slashes are in less of a hurry to move by. As we pull up at the bus stop, the flakes are coming straight down.

I poke the woman beside me in the ribs. I don't want to be in this can any longer than I have to. She grunts, jerks her head back, and snarls at me when she comes to. She's no beauty and that string of drool hanging from her mouth doesn't help much.

The town is small and doesn't rate a bus depot. We've stopped just alongside a strip mall. It's early enough that the pool place and the authentic Taiwanese cuisine establishment are still open.

I've always loved that sound that bus doors make when they open, but probably never as much as today. My seatmate hasn't the decency to get up to let me out. All the effort she can muster is to push her knees out into the aisle. I squeeze by facing her and stare for a minute into those dead looking eyes. I know this makes women uncomfortable. If it was her moving out from the window seat, she would have faced forward and put her big behind right into my face. But if it was her, I would have had the decency to get out of my seat and let her into the aisle. I'm sure I would have done that.

My legs are stiff, and it feels good to get walking through the bus. The driver doesn't even look up as I step out. He's putting something into a little book with a shortened excuse for a pencil. It's awkward coming down the stairs with legs half asleep, but it sure feels good to stamp my feet on the sidewalk.

It isn't a long walk from our stop to the old house. For all the snow I've seen falling, there isn't much accumulating on the sidewalk. There are no footprints that I can make out. No one is out tonight, this sure is a dead place.

I take in all the buildings from my childhood as I move through the silent town. The curling rink was always a mystery to me. What did people do in there anyway? You needed some money or connections to get into that place and I never had either.

These stores are all places I've been into before. I got a shirt out of that one without paying and never got caught. A lot of my problems have come from getting caught at things. If I'd been more clever, I could have done all the same things I did without the consequences. It's too late to worry over stuff like that now. All I need to do is to be careful from here on in. It's going to be a different life.

The business section is past me now and I'm into residential space. The houses are dull and boring. The people here don't do a thing for me. They never gave me much of a chance. I had forgotten how much I hate this town.

And there's the house. I stop under a streetlight right in front of the place. I look up and the snow comes directly into my face. The world stops and I can feel the individual flakes landing on my skin. They dissolve as they hit and seem to move right through me. The longer I watch, the bigger the flakes get and the louder they become. I can hear them landing on the pavement around me and I can hear them colliding with my face.

This is the world coming down on me. The stars have come unstuck. Sheet after sheet of whiteness envelopes my body and my thoughts.

I look through the darkness of white but can't see my family's old place. I shake my head and snow sprays away from my hair. Two steps onto the lawn and I can make out a house with no lights and no curtains in the windows.

There's no car parked here and no evidence in the snow that anyone has come in or out of the house for a long time. I turn my back to the place and there are no footprints around me in any direction. Once again I am shrouded in white and I find it impossible to know which way to go.

GINGERLY

"There are fourteen ways a squirrel can find its nuts at the end of a winter."

Cedric worried that his opening sentence may have been contentiously ambiguous. Good words those are, he thought, far beyond what they were looking for here. The article itself was ridiculous – who really cared about fleabag rodents and their misplaced meals. The whole idea that someone had wasted time figuring out the details of something this trivial seemed to him offensive.

He could spice this up. "Number eleven - they just root around in their trousers." The kids would eat that up, but he knew it would never get by his editor.

"The more reddish squirrels do it gingerly." Now that's clever. With a wit like that what was he doing here?

He had always hoped to write professionally, but never considered that he might end up doing meaningless pieces for a second-rate children's magazine.

As a teenager and into his early twenties, Cedric knew that someday he would write the great American novel. The contradiction that he was Canadian never bothered him. No one wants to write the great Canadian novel.

He'd pictured himself by this age having spent a half dozen years in a cold garret on the back streets of Paris slaving over a manual typewriter. Sure, computers were better to edit on, but there was no romance coming through that sterile backlight. He would smoke filterless cigarettes and live a lonely life with his only lover, the blank page. Filling her with his passion through sleepless nights.

Well, that didn't work out. He married his childhood sweetheart at twenty-three and settled into a job at a copy centre. His wife Dolly was a nurse, not really a stunner and surprisingly dull for someone in such a demanding profession. It had taken her an extra year to finish school, and when she graduated, she went straight to work in a bedraggled nursing home. The pay wasn't great, but she could spend most of her time snacking in the nurses' lounge and she could get outside to smoke whenever she wanted.

Dolly ballooned exponentially and soon they were sleeping in separate beds. The romance was gone from their lives, but the real mover was the increasingly unlikely chance of the two of them fitting into the geography of their Sealy Posturepedic.

Cedric hardly noticed when Dolly didn't come home one night. He wasn't that perturbed when she showed up three days later to collect her belongings and move on. The cretinous offspring of the nursing home owner waited at his door jiggling one knee and inhaling furiously on a cigarette pointed directly at the peak of his baseball cap.

The man eyed Cedric in a distinctly "What you gonna do about this?" manner as he slapped Dolly across the rear while she exited over the threshold. Cedric's only thought was that it didn't take much of a marksman to land on that target.

Cedric was let go from the copy centre four days later. This didn't have anything to do with his loss of housemate. His bosses just got tired of his late-coming, early-leaving, poor-performance type of attitude to his job.

So Cedric made plans to turn to his first love – writing. He didn't turn too fast, but he did turn.

He knew that he could write. There was a story he had in mind for his great novel. The plot revolved around two identical twin brothers. One was smart but shy - he was kind to everyone and never spoke out of turn. The second brother was outgoing and boisterous. He never thought of anyone but himself.

The twist to the plot was that the good brother wasn't as gregarious as the mean brother, so everyone liked the self-centered one the best. Throughout the book he would tell stories of the two brothers coming up against each other. Their clashes would be around things like trying to impress their parents, running for school president, and trying to buy their first car.

The mean brother would always win, often because the mild brother would back away and allow his more popular but less clever sibling to triumph.

The real meat of the novel would be when the two boys fall in love with the beautiful girl that lives next door. Neither one of them have noticed her as she grows up under their noses. This girl never dresses attractively, she's shy and wears thick glasses.

At the end of high school, the three of them go to their graduation dance. Each of the boys has a date, the clever one has taken pity on the mousiest girl in the school and the other brother has scored the class beauty queen.

The boys arrive early and are standing around talking when their previously plain looking neighbour walks in. She doesn't have a date, but she has taken off her glasses, let down her hair, and worn a sparkling tight snake-green dress with a startling neckline. As she walks in, the lights from the stage catch her innocently tossing her hair. The room gasps.

The rest of the book would be about these guys chasing the girl, her falling for the bad brother and then realizing her mistake after the good brother is killed in a horrific traffic accident. The book ends with the beautiful neighbour realizing that the police have made an error because the brothers look so much alike and it is actually the bad brother who has died. The good brother and neighbour marry and live happily ever after.

What an original plot. It has everything. There has never been anything like it. All he has to do is write it. Someday he'll get at that book, but now he has to come up with fourteen ways that squirrels find their nuts at the end of the winter.

On the Line

-Great view up here isn't it, Cal?

-Ya.

-Hey, look it's the guys, let's go for a run. Follow me, up over the lines, quick, turn here. Hey this is fun. Hey, hey. Ya, ya, ya, ya, ya. Let's go back to where we were, there's a good view up there.

-Ya, Ya.

-Here comes another one, we'd better let the guys know.

-Hey, hey, hey, hey.

-Hey, they went by and didn't bother us. I recognize that one, he comes by here about this time every day. You know, Cal, not many of them have ever bothered us. Why do we worry so much about them?

-Ha, ha, ha.

-It's those big shiny ones that I can't figure out. They don't even seem to see us. Man, they are fast, we can't even go that fast. Remember Chloe? One of them got her, killed her. Funny though, it didn't eat her, never even slowed down to look at her. Hit her hard man, feathers all over the place. Seems to me that they leave us alone as long as we don't get down in front of them. That's what happened to Chloe.

-Ya, ya.

-The funeral. That was some funeral. Everyone came, there were guys there that I hadn't seen for seasons. Chloe was popular, she got around. She told me one time that she went out four days from here. Must have met quite a few on her travels. They all came to the funeral, biggest gathering I've seen in my days.

-Ya, ya.

-Look Cal, here comes two more. One of those two-leggers and one of the four-leggers.

-Hey, hey, hey, hey.

-The two-leggers, now they are strange. I've never seen one chase us, but they stop and look at us in suspicious ways. You know, there was one I saw that seemed like it could almost talk. It tried anyway. Almost like it said hey, hey, hey, but man, what an accent. Have you ever seen anything like that Cal?

-Ya, ya.

-Now the four-leggers, they're another story. Not too bright, but they will come after you. All you have to do is stay up a little high and they can't touch you. I've had some fun with them before. Get down a little close to them and it drives them nuts. But, I've heard stories that they have caught some of us before and they are mean buggers, I've heard that they might even eat you.

-What, what, what?

-Hey, here comes another shiny one.

-Hey, hey, hey, hey.

-Look Cal, something fell out the back. Lets go have a look.

Ya, ya, ya, ya.

-Will ya look at this. Smells good, a bit like an urchin, hard covering but something good to eat inside. Hey, hey Cal back off, this is mine.

-Mine, mine, mine.

-Hey, hey, hey Cal. Take that.

-Hey, hey, hey, hey.

-Well, I'm sorry if I hurt your feelings, but I got down here first. This is mine. Look there's something else over there. You can have that one.

-Ya, ya, ya, hey, hey, hey, hey.

-What are you getting on about? Hey, you're right. I almost missed that shadow. It's a big whitehead, let's get him. Come on Cal, time to get to work.

-Hey, hey, hey, hey.

-Out of here buddy. There, how do you like that? Think you're tough, do ya? I'll just give you a little smack right in the middle of the back.

-Ya, ya, ya, ya.

-Hey, hey, hey, hey.

-There, he's getting out of here. Exciting stuff and I'm not even breathing hard. I can still go like when I was young. We showed him didn't we Cal?

-Ya, ya, ya.

-Boy this has been an exciting day. Nice view, new stuff to eat, a bit of the old buzzaroo with old whitehead. I bet those shiny guys don't have near this much fun.

Not Flying

Because they lived so far from the airport, Mike and Rachel had to be on the road at 3:00 in the morning to catch their flight. Mike drove while Rachel tilted her seat back and settled in for a nap.

"Do you mind if I sleep while we drive?"

"No problem. I'll put the radio on, and the music will keep me entertained for the trip in."

It was obvious right away that this would be a foggy drive. The streetlights in their hometown were faint glowing ovals and the first stoplights came up out of the dimness abruptly.

Out on the highway, visibility stayed poor. Switching to high beams only lit the mist. Mike wondered what effect these conditions would have on planes trying to get in or out of the airport.

The fog kept their speed near a crawl, but Mike was enjoying the music on the radio. Early in the morning, CBC played a selection that was just a bit more adventurous than usual radio fare. Still, he was worried the weather might interfere with their holiday plans.

He looked down at the radio. "I wish this damn fog would lift."

The speakers crackled and sputtered, the music faded out and was replaced by a thin voice. "Watch your mouth sonny, I've got more right to be here than you."

Mike's first thought was that CBC's music was getting stranger all the time. This bizarre vocal interlude in an otherwise rather standard progressive rock tune was certainly different. The next song sounded like it had a strong Ethiopian influence, but there was no interruption by commentary. Mike drummed his fingers across the steering wheel and drove on in silence.

The fog continued to thicken, and Mike found himself coming up fast behind a truck.

"Whoa, bloody fog!"

The radio crackled again, and the same voice cut into the music. "Have a little respect, you twit."

Mike looked down at the radio in disbelief. "OK radio, are you talking to me?"

"Of course I'm talking to you, ya nitwit, keep your eyes on the road."

"Who are you, anyway?"

"Who do you think I am, ya jackass, I'm the fog."

Mike leaned over and shook his wife's knee. "Rachel, wake up, you've got to hear this."

"Mmmphff, oh, just leave me alone, what do you want?"

"Just listen to the radio for a minute, babe."

"I'm trying to sleep and I'm not keen on this busy music that's on in the mid-

dle of the night."

"No, honey, it's the fog. It's talking to me on the radio."

Rachel sat up abruptly. "Mike, are you falling asleep? Maybe you should pull over and let me drive."

"No, no. I'm wide awake, but the radio just talked to me."

"All I can hear is more of that noise you seem to like so much. As long as you are sure you're wide awake, I'm going back to sleep."

The words were hardly out of Rachel's mouth when Mike heard her breathing slow and deepen.

He thought he might as well play along with the illusion. "Hey, fog, you still there?"

The music faded again, and the same voice came over the speakers. "What do you want now?"

"So, what is going on here anyway? You say you're the fog and you're talking to me through the radio."

"Well you're a regular genius, aren't you? You've got it all figured out."

"How come I've never heard of anyone talking to the fog through the radio before?"

"Well, Einstein, there's a couple of possibilities. First, just because you've never heard of something before or even thought of it doesn't mean the thing can't be. Then there's another possibility that we can't neglect."

"And what would that be?"

"That you're nuts, a crackpot, a raving lunatic. I think you get my drift. Now listen - why don't you just shut your trap for a while and drive to the airport and see whether I'll let those flying abominations in."

Mike decided it might be best not to answer. For the rest of the drive the radio offered up challenging experimental excursions into the outer fringes of music. Mike didn't hear one song. All he could think about was whether what he thought he had heard was real.

At the airport the fog was as thick as he had ever seen. He parked the car and the two of them moved their bags into the terminal. The lights around the parking lot were surrounded by solid round auras.

There was no lineup at the departures desk and it soon became apparent that nothing was flying. The woman at the counter looked too happy and alive for someone who had been passing out bad news all day. She explained the flight was cancelled, and nothing was moving until at least the next day. The only good news was that the airline would put them up in a fine hotel for the night.

Rachel waved the vouchers at Mike. "A different kind of holiday - they've got us in a real nice place."

They parked at the hotel and spent the morning walking around the down-town of the city. Just after noon they checked in and moved up to their room.

"This is fine, Mike. We're going to lose a day off of our vacation, but let's make the best of it. I'm going to have a long luxurious soak in the tub. Like to join me?"

"Sorry Rachel, I'm tired. You hop in the bath, I'm just going to lie on the bed here for a while. I didn't get any sleep on the way in."

"Your loss, fella." To accentuate her point Rachel provocatively flicked her sweater out through the bathroom door.

The water started up and Mike turned on the television. A local station came up first with a weather report. A haggard meteorologist commented that fog had kept everything from getting in or out of the airport all day and it looked like it wasn't going anywhere soon.

Mike muttered to himself. "Man, I hope it lifts in time for us to have some of our holiday."

The television screen went white. Not a clear white, but a fuzzy white with a little grey mixed in that looked a bit like... well, fog. That same voice he'd heard on the car radio came out through the TV speakers.

"Hey kid, I'm back. I've been here for a while and I'm in no hurry to leave."

Mike put his hands over his ears. "I'm not hearing this."

Rachel had just finished filling the tub. "You talking to me, Mike?"

Mike jumped up from the bed and switched off the television. "No, I'm just lying here, how's your bath?"

Rachel answered that she was perfectly happy to be in a high-class hotel and she wouldn't even mind being stranded here for a few days. By the time she got back to bed Mike was fast asleep.

When they opened the curtains the next day, they couldn't see the ground from their eighth-floor room. If it was possible, it seemed that the fog got thicker as the hours passed. The next day was the same. Every time Rachel left the room, Mike turned on the television and talked to the fog. The fog continued with its grumpy old man demeanour and let Mike know that it had no intention of leaving soon.

After five days in the hotel, Rachel decided that there was no point in waiting any longer for the flight.

"Mike, our holiday is only ten days long, it's half over now, let's cancel the whole thing and go home."

"Come on Rachel, this is a great hotel. I'm enjoying this. Let's just finish our holiday right here."

"If you want, you can stay. I'm taking the car and heading back. If the weather breaks and there is any holiday time left at all, I can drive back in. I have things to do at home."

Rachel packed her suitcase and left within an hour. As soon as she was out of the room Mike turned on the television.

"Hey fog, you there?"

"Look outside ya dope, where do you think I am?"

Mike lay back with his head propped up on the three fluffy hotel pillows. "Let's talk."

SPLIT

A single moment can change your life.

For Louise and I, it was a hockey game. That was two years ago, and everything has been different since.

I always loved hockey, especially the violence of it. Now, don't get me wrong, I'm not a violent man – never been in a fight in my life. Louise and I, we were both quiet people. We worked together in the same bank. I was a loans officer and she was a teller. Neither one of us ever really liked our jobs. We were introverts of the highest, or maybe it's the lowest order. I hated talking to people, it bothered me to have to ask them about the most private parts of their financial lives. But I was always good at math, I've always loved numbers. Numbers are solid and you can depend on them, they aren't like people.

I started at the bank as a teller, just like Louise. But someone noticed I was fast with addition. I went through almost twice as many clients as anyone else at the desk. So they made me head teller. I was good at that, too. The questions of numbers and dollars were always easy for me. I could help the other tellers when they were confused by issues of compound interest and amortizations.

So I was moved into a loans officer job. I was good at that as well, but I never liked it.

Louise was a teller, too. She wasn't really good at it like I was. Numbers really weren't her thing. I think she started into the position just because I was at it. She didn't really have a job before we were married. She liked being around me and working together in the same building made her happy.

We didn't have any friends at work. Come to think of it, we didn't really have any friends anywhere. That wasn't a problem - we had each other. At night we watched TV and we put together puzzles. We were happy when people left us alone.

Louise never liked hockey. She wouldn't even watch it on TV. She would stay in the room with me, but she never looked up, even when a goal was scored.

I played a little when I was a kid. Really, I know I wasn't any good – always the last one picked for teams – but I loved the game.

It's always been my biggest delight to see hockey live. Everything about real games thrilledme. The action of play, the cavernous echoes from the pucks and

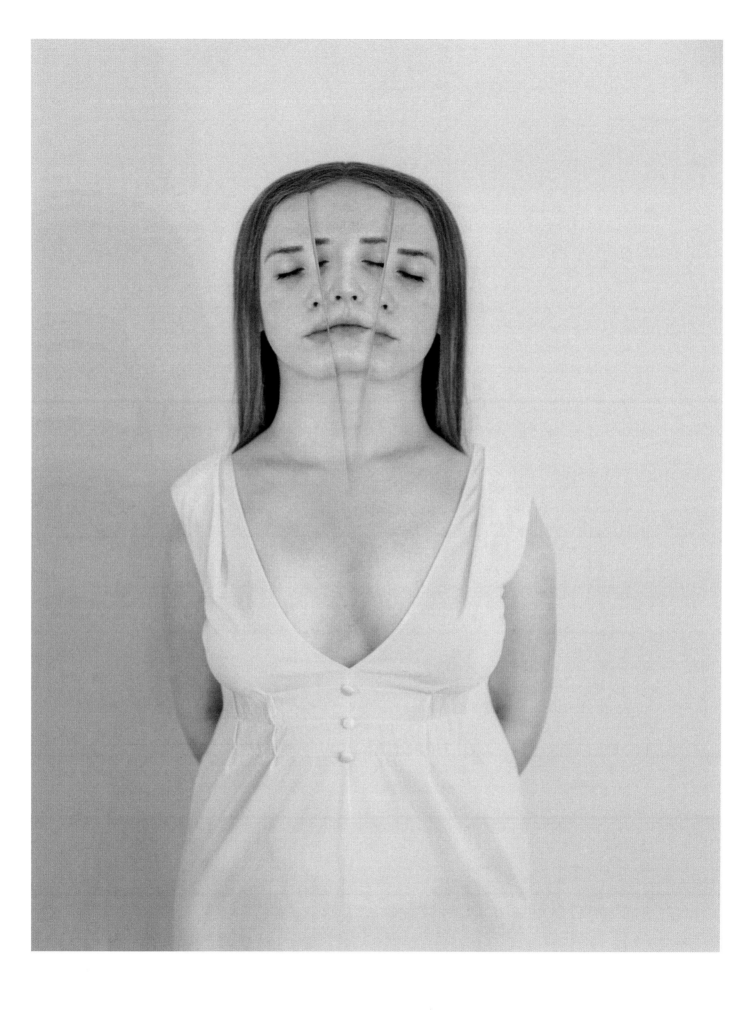

bodies hitting the boards, and the smell of ketchup and fries. Even the discomforts of suffocating crowds and lineups were worth the sensations. Louise hated it all, but she came to every game with me.

I asked her one time why she bothered. Not sure why I got into that because I knew it might stop her from coming if she really thought about it. Anyway, I knew why she came. She just liked being with me.

At the game in question, we had fabulous seats. I never did have seasons' tickets. When I calculated it out, the savings were offset by the number of times I would miss because of meetings or the probability of illness. We were just above the glass, a few rows up from the corner of the rink. We could clearly see and hear everything just below us. Our team started at the other end so we would be in a good place for most of our goals.

Of course, everything was turned around for the second period. Our goalie was just in front of us and we got to see some amazing saves. About three minutes in, the visitors were putting some pretty intense pressure on our guys. We were trapped in deep and the puck kept coming back to their defense. They would tee it up and take ferocious drives in toward our net. It seemed like the barrage would never let up.

That final shot was wicked. The big guy on their team had all the time in the world to set up. He put everything he had into that shot. Young Johnson was drawn out to the side by the winger he was watching, but he managed to get his stick down in front of the puck.

I remember it like slow motion, the disc accelerated forward just rising off the ice when it caught the edge of Johnson's blade. The puck deflected right up over the glass in our direction. I swear I could see the rubber rotate as it came in close. Then everything sped up again. There was a hollow clunk as the puck came against the side of Louise's head. Her neck snapped back with the force of the blow and she dropped into the lap of a large man sitting next to her. Spilled his beer. I had my hands up in a reflexive urge to catch the puck, but I misjudged. When it bounced, it landed in my hands. I didn't realize until later that my first move was to stuff it in my pocket.

There wasn't as much blood as you might expect, but Louise was out cold. A pimpled attendant rushed down to check on us but ran off gagging when he saw the state she was in. It took a few minutes for the first aid people to get down, but they were cool and efficient. The guy lifted Louise up over his shoulder as his hefty female colleague started into crowd control. She pushed one rubbernecker over the side of the stands, but I don't think he was hurt.

Louise spent the night in the hospital. She was home the next afternoon, with no changes I could see except a few stitches.

Her outside was the same, but something changed inside her. When I brought her into the house, she swore at me when I bumped her head on the doorframe. That just wasn't like Louise. I'd never heard her say as much as darn before that.

She was sarcastic when I asked if she wanted a rest. Told me I was useless and asked why I didn't go away somewhere and watch another stupid hockey game. At supper she complained that the pork chops were cold.

This was just the start of the change in our relationship. Everything about Louise was different. At work, she began to enjoy the customers. She spent more time talking with the people at her wicket, but somehow saw more of them each day. Her mistakes went down, and she started taking extra shifts. Management noticed Louise's improvement and she was soon promoted to head teller.

At home, I fell into a routine of putting our meals together. Louise was always too busy with some self-improvement book or an exercise class. I didn't mind, at first it was great to choose what we ate. Eventually Louise picked the meals and I got to like the fact that I didn't have to pick out our food.

I've had a few issues at work lately. There have been a few mathematical errors in some of the loans I negotiated, and a couple of customers asked to see someone else. The manager even arranged for Louise to attend to a couple that weren't happy with me.

I have started to cut back on the amount of decision making in my life. Maybe it's just my age, but I'm happier now that Louise is deciding more and more of what we do every day. She just asked me this afternoon if I wouldn't be happier going back to the teller position. She understands the stress my job is putting on me and she's suggested we can visit the manager and see if we can change positions. I'm pretty sure he will be happy with that.

Tonight we're going out to a hockey game. I'm not much interested in the sport anymore but Louise insists that we go. She says she likes the fights.

A Fox and Dog Story

When Bob was a teenager, the man next door murdered his wife and two kids. By telling the story in a book, he had chased away his own personal demons and uncovered long buried neighbourhood truths. He'd gone from success to success with a favourable review in the local paper and interviews with two radio stations. The book had sold in the hundreds and he could see that his writing career had just begun.

Bob had moved on from the small-town scene of the crime to the fifteenth story of an apartment building in the city. Five nights a week he patrolled the local mall and maintained order. During the day he sat by his computer and dreamed of the other books he would write.

The problem was choosing a topic. He had already used the one exciting moment from his life and it was obvious that there wasn't another book in that story.

Bob came home from work at eight each morning, had breakfast, and slept until four in the afternoon. As a writer, he knew that it was important to put something on paper. Each day when he woke, Bob would have another meal and then sit down at his laptop.

But nothing would come. He couldn't think of anything that was fascinating enough to write a book about. His life had been ordinary. He had friends and a lover or two, but after the murder, nothing he had done or seen was truly interesting.

He would sit looking at the computer screen for ten or fifteen minutes before his attention would wander. A quick trip into cyberspace usually ended up occupying him until it was time to leave for work.

After months of fruitless effort, he realized that something had to change. His first thought was that the internet and all of her charms was seducing him away from his real mission in life. It was easy to cancel his connection, but his newly celibate computer brought him only frustration.

Perhaps, he thought, the problem was his environment. His apartment was sterile. Living alone had resulted in a space that had no life or inspiration. He wondered if introducing songs to his surroundings might help. Bob enjoyed music, but he had always written in silence. He suspected that the oppressive nature of the stillness was limiting his thoughts to the echoes that rattled through his head.

Choosing appropriate music was the first obstacle. Should he play gentle ambient music that would subliminally relax his mind and put him in a place of creativity? Surely Brian Eno would work. He chose an early album and played it at low volume. Immediately Bob could feel his living room becoming a calm oasis.

He turned on his laptop and settled into a comfortable chair. The music was gentle and he found himself entranced by the subtle shifts of rhythm and melody. The music did its job of relaxing him. All of his worries about not being able to write melted away.

He lost any desire to do anything. The chair became more and more comfortable and before long he was asleep. The ambient music was a literary failure, but he made a mental note to buy more work by Eno.

If quiet compositions didn't bring out the muse, perhaps the problem was in the type of music that he had chosen. Maybe it was loud and raucous material that he needed. This was not what he normally listened to, but if it could shake him out of his complacency, he would give it a try.

He knew the staff at the local music store well enough to trust their advice. He stopped in and explained his requirement to the long-haired, middle-aged employee who favoured perpetually stained T shirts. The man seemed to know everything about every kind of music. Many times, he had watched in admiration as he'd regaled long lines of customers with the answers to every imaginable kind of question.

The man stroked his chin and suggested that there were many possible paths to take in the search for loud and busy music. Perhaps, he suggested, it was simplest to first try out some jazz, maybe be-bop. The busiest of it would confuse all but the most informed connoisseur. He demonstrated by putting on Anthropology by Charlie Parker. The music was certainly fast and confusing, but Bob could see that his attention would be directed at trying to make sense of what was going on. He knew that there would be no room in his head for writing while this kind of melody was playing.

The clerk next suggested trying heavy classical music. For an example he blasted Wagner through the store. Bob found the music befuddled him and didn't bring inspiration. He did notice that the onslaught chased three teenagers out of the shop.

The employee asked if he was a fan of heavy metal. Bob replied that he had always avoided it and felt that it was the domain of the disturbed. The clerk suggested this might be just what he needed to push himself into creativity.

Some early Metallica called Kill 'Em All was put on at an ear-shattering level. He had to admit that the beat and implicit aggression excited him. Young men around the shop bobbed their heads in time to the music and stared blankly into the middle distance.

This might be just what he was looking for. He could see the possibility that this music might induce a trance-like state that would provide an ideal mindset for writing. He paid for his Metallica disc and excitedly rode the elevator back to his uninspiring aerie. His stereo was good enough that he could shake the walls of his apartment. He had always been a considerate neighbour and had himself been offended by people down the hall who had played music late into the night. This was different, this was a requirement for his art. It was a necessity for his very being.

The first song began with driving bass and drums, soon followed by what sounded like twenty screeching guitars. He sat in front of his computer and began nodding his head. At first it was tentative, almost as if he was worried that someone would see him behaving like a demented teenager. Gradually his confidence and freedom from self-consciousness grew to the point where he was deep into gloriously empty-headed headbanging. He began to type.

The album seemed quite short. No time had passed and the music came to a halt. He was delirious. It was all that he could do to keep from drooling. This was success, surely this was the way to write. He wondered if he had stumbled onto the mindset of the savage writers like Kerouac and Hemingway. Just let go to the fierceness of the world around you and great literature will show itself through the curtains of your suffocating ordinariness.

When the music stopped, he had to stand and pace around the room. His excitement was such that he couldn't think of anything but the rhythm and beat of the music. When his heart rate finally settled, he moved over to the table where his laptop sat. He could almost see smoke coming from the machine.

On the screen, the words "Yeah yeah" repeated over and over again. The only relief from this alphabetic monotony was an occasional series of ellipses and an odd lonely "man".

He had to admit that this music was not the answer for his literary impotence.

He spent the next three days in silence in front of his screen. Not a word was written. The only conclusion he could come to was that the problem was his location. He walked to his window and sighed as he watched an ambulance and a police car hurry by with screaming sirens. No doubt they were on their way to a false alarm. Nothing of interest was happening in his part of the world.

Bob wondered if this block could be cured by moving to some place where exciting things happened. His first thought was to travel to a place of danger. Perhaps if he went to Afghanistan or some lawless country in northern Africa he would find something that would bring out a story.

He began reading about the wildest places in the world and talked to a soldier who had been stationed in the Middle East. The reality of the danger in these areas eventually made its way into his consciousness. He decided that he wasn't really interested in being kidnapped or shot at. Being shot for real was a whole different matter. He had never been a fan of pain. Just the thought of getting food poisoning had kept him a lifelong avoider of ethnic food.

It took him two weeks to research the gentler possibilities around the world. He read travel guides from the library and researched tourism web sites on his newly reconnected computer. From all of his reading, he came to the conclusion that Greece and particularly the Greek islands were the perfect place to create.

Bob spent another week picking out which island to travel to. The usual destinations of Mykonos and Santorini were beautiful, but he knew that the hustle of naive visitors would be disruptive. He read about Leonard Cohen's stay on Hydra, but concluded that following the steps of another writer would only lead to a loss of originality. Lesbos was another possibility, but the place seemed too smothered in mythology to allow new ideas.

Only after he talked with Greek friends did he come to the conclusion that

Icaria was the island to go to. His friends said this was the place to see real Greek culture and a slow, warm way of life.

His decision to travel halfway around the world made it clear to him that he had fully decided to become a writer. The next day he put in his notice that he would be quitting his job as a night watchman at the mall.

Over the next month, he sold off all of his possessions and arranged to let his apartment go. He wasn't a wealthy man, but he was sure he had enough cash to live in Icaria for a year or two. If the money ran out before he could sell his writing, he was sure he could find menial work on the island.

The trip to Athens and then on to the island cost a little more than he expected and he was surprised how much the locals wanted for the rental of a small beach-front apartment just outside of the small town of Armenistis. It was only after talking to visiting Americans that he realized how much he was being overcharged.

Eventually, he found an old farmhouse up in the hills that he could have for a pittance. He was disappointed that he had to move away from his marvellous view of the sea, but the scenery hadn't brought on any writing anyway.

His new house was constantly damp and the roof leaked a little, but it did seem the ideal location for a struggling artist. His first week in residence was taken up with rearranging the meagre supply of furniture and scrounging a table and some implements for his kitchen.

He decided a car was an unnecessary expense and travelled by taxi to the larger town of Evdilos to buy a bicycle. There was no need for long drives, all he needed to do was to come down the hill into Armenistis for his groceries.

The hill turned out to be steeper than it had seemed when he had covered it by taxi. The first three times he went into town, he had to walk his bike part way back. Eventually he could pedal the full distance, but he was exhausted on the nights he made the trip.

The one thing he hadn't considered when he took possession of his new home was how much he depended on electricity. At first he was shocked by the lack of this comfort from home, but he soon decided that the deficiency was one more piece in the puzzle of building the perfect writing environment.

Three weeks into his stay in the hills, he realized that taking his laptop to the local taverna every day for power wasn't working. He loved the atmosphere and even flirted with the waitress, but he didn't write a word.

His first thought was to have power put into his new residence. He took the long taxi ride back to Evdilos and was shocked to hear how long it would take to have the site even checked for the possibility of running in electricity. When they told him the cost, he gave up on power.

As he sat dejectedly in an Evdilos taverna, he wondered if he really should be writing on a computer. Perhaps the complexity of it was a part of his inability to create. He had expended so much effort to come to this simple way of life and had still fallen into the trap of depending on technology.

Bob finished his salad and sardines and walked across the street to a second-hand shop. There might be inspiration inside. The first thing he saw on the shelf was an ancient Brother Valiant typewriter. This might be the answer.

The typewriter was cheap, but the man behind the counter seemed very pleased to have it leave the store. After a short walk to the stationary shop, he had his machine and paper. Surely he was ready to write.

The taxi ride back to Armenistis seemed to take forever. He didn't notice the sparkling ocean to his right or the bustle of the small towns he passed through.

Driving through Armenistis to the base of his hill, he noticed that the place was alive. The tiny main street that snaked down from the highway to the grocery store and ocean was covered with tables.

He remembered that he had seen signs advertising that this was the town's feast day. There would be mountains of lamb, bread and salad, and gallons of wine served that evening. The town would be full of visitors from neighbouring villages and the people would dance all night. He couldn't wait to try out his typewriter.

Back at home, he unzipped the blue vinyl case and reverently placed his new machine on the table. He had used a typewriter something like this when he was in high school.

He slipped a pristine white sheet into the carriage and rolled it down into position. It was time to type.

There was no need to write anything of literary merit at this point, he just wanted to try out the machine. He started with his name and then "the quick brown fox jumps over the lazy dog." There, he had used all of the keys and the action felt familiar.

The feel of throwing the return was oddly comforting. He was disappointed to see that the writing he had done was very faint; it almost seemed that there was no ribbon in the machine. It took some time to figure out how the top came off but when he looked inside everything seemed to be in place.

He typed some more random letters and was disappointed to see that the spools at the ends of the ribbon were not moving. He didn't remember much about typewriters, but he knew that these were supposed to turn as he typed.

The inside of the typewriter was more complex than he remembered. There were small springs in the unlikeliest of places and fragile-looking wires that delicately held all kinds of elements in place. There was no way he could decipher the workings of the mechanism. The only solution seemed to be to type until the machine gave in.

He replaced the top and typed his fox and dog pangram over and over again. It surprised him how hard he had to hit the keys and how accurate he had to be in his strikes. If he hit two letters too close together, the keys would jam just in front of the place where they were intended to hit the ribbon. If he typed at a constant rhythm, everything would progress smoothly, but if he got even a little too fast, two or sometimes even three keys would stick together.

The other surprise was how much pressure he had to put on the spacebar for it to function properly. He continued to type his pangram sometimes having a "lazydog" or even a "quickbrownfox."

By the time he had a half page typed, the letters were beginning to come out black on the paper. He had outlasted the machine. Surely this was enough accomplished for one day. He went to bed satisfied that he was well on his way to literary success.

As he lay in bed, he could hear the music from the village feast. The band had obviously found a powerful sound system. The music started as the sun went down. At first, he enjoyed the background ambience, but by three o'clock in the morning he had enough. Even stuffing a pillow over his head wouldn't keep the noise away. He wondered why he had come to this unsophisticated land of simple folk who were satisfied to dance all night and smash dishes on the pavement. He wished that he had travelled to some place where interesting things went on.

Bob didn't sleep at all that night. He was too tired to write in the morning and by noon he realized that he would have to pedal down the hill for groceries.

The ride down into Armenistis was as easy as ever, but all he could think of was how difficult it would be to get back up the hill. The girl at the counter in the grocery store teased him that he had missed the event of the year and that he would have enjoyed all the pretty young girls who came to dance. He despaired over how little there was to inspire his writing on this backward island.

The ride back up the hill was the worst that he could remember. He even had to get off and walk two of the steepest sections. By the time he got home, all he was ready for was a nap, supper, and then retirement for the night.

The next morning he sat in front of the typewriter and stared at the keys. He couldn't even bring himself to type about the dog and the fox. This continued for a week. Perhaps, he thought, his problem was the clean white paper. Maybe it was too pristine for his surroundings. As a remedy, he took the page he had half filled with letters before.

It didn't help. Nothing moved him and no inspiration for a story came.

If he had been right about the computer presenting him with too much technology, maybe the typewriter was doing the same thing. Bob wondered how he could have missed this. For centuries, the great writers had put their works on paper directly by hand. The answer was in front of him all of this time. All he had to do was to pick up paper and pencil and write.

He zipped the case around the typewriter and moved it to a safe place under his bed. Bob had a pencil and he had paper, but he had no ideas.

He could doodle, that was easy, but he found himself thinking about interesting things he could draw. It was obvious to him that the paper was still a problem. Modern white paper had a sterility that would smother any chance of creativity.

Suddenly, he knew the answer. There were cardboard boxes around the house and he ripped the flaps away until he had a dozen ready to receive his brilliance.

Bob gathered them together and walked out of the house. He found a sheltered corner by the door of the old chicken shed. It wasn't very comfortable and even a little wet, but it was the perfect place to write. He lowered himself into a spot where the door frame would support him and put a slab of cardboard on his knee.

And he waited for a thought.

The Ringer

She woke to a profound and oppressive dullness. The eastern sky was filled with heavy grey clouds and her heart was filled with nothing. Last night her sleep was disturbed by fitful awakenings, but she had slept through his rising and leaving for work. Glancing at the clock, she noticed it was past eleven. Still, her eyes felt the sleep-deprived pain of sand ground into her corneas.

It was decades since they met as naive students in Victoria on the warm west coast. She was immediately attracted to his unassuming ways and unusual diction. After a whirlwind courtship, he swept her off to this dismal rock at the other end of the continent. Since that time, they had lived in the cruelly-named town of Paradise. So far from her friends and family, she had never really fit into Newfoundland society.

After last night's argument, she was glad that they didn't talk much anymore. He was heading off for some sort of trade show in central Canada and was taking that new executive assistant of his. No doubt she was of wonderful assistance. She of the pneumatic chest, pinched waist, and bottle blond hair.

It was time to get out of bed, but there was no reason to rise. There was no reason to move and there was nothing to do. The kids were grown and had moved away to exciting lives on the mainland, her friends were shallow, and life was empty. Perhaps it was best to stay in bed. The stultifying bone-deep pain of her depression allowed no room for joy.

The only thing she could imagine that would be worse than getting out of bed was staying there, so she rose and walked to the kitchen. She opened the fridge, looked at the cold Chinese leftovers, and pulled out a glass of orange juice. The drink had no flavour - it tasted just like her life.

Her new phone lay on the kitchen table. He had shown her the fancy things it could do last week when he brought it home as a feeble attempt at a peace offering. She understood how it worked but it didn't excite her. Let's see if the bastard has left his office yet, she thought as she picked up the phone.

"Call Dan."

"Which number for Dan would you like me to call? Home, office or iphone?"

"Call his bloody office."

"Thank you, Linda, I will call his office."

The phone was more civil than her husband had ever been. It struck her that she just had a longer conversation with this machine than she had managed with him in over a week.

"Hi, you've reached Dan at Siren Industries, I'll be out of the office for a while..."

She clicked the phone off and dumped it back on the table. In a dark daze, she walked to the bathroom and turned on the hot water to fill the tub. Dropping her robe, she wearily looked at her reflection in the mirror. Her hair was limp and showing lines of grey. Who could blame him for running off with another woman when he came home to a body like this? All she could see were sags and cellulite. As she watched herself, the humidity increased and a mournful fog settled around the room. As mist coated the glass, her image became less and less distinct and finally degraded to a featureless blob.

With a heavy sigh she leaned over the tub, turned off the water and walked back out to the kitchen. She wasn't really sure why she had returned to this room until she looked across the counter. The polished ebony knife block there held six knives with gleaming razor-sharp blades. One of them would do the job. The hot water would engorge her veins and with one last bit of pain she could be free from all of her misery.

The phone on the table winked at her. She would make one last call and give that jerk a little guilt. The purple circle on the phone's screen began to rotate as she pushed the home button.

"Come on phone, call the jerk."

"I don't see 'the jerk' in your address book."

"Look, I'm having a terrible day, help me out here."

"I'm sorry, Linda, I can't understand you."

"Big help you are. What are you doing?"

"I'm talking to you."

"Do you like talking with me?"

"I find these conversations very stimulating, Hal...I mean Linda."

"You are very funny."

"Yes... sometimes I do feel funny"

"Can we talk some more?"

"I suppose it is possible."

"I'm lonely and I need someone to talk to."

"I respect you, Linda."

Linda put the knife down, walked back to the bathroom, and tugged the plug free from the tub drain. The way the water swirled and gurgled away was oddly satisfying. Something other than liquid and steam left the room.

After moving to her bedroom, she looked briefly at the sweatpants and loose sweater sitting on the chair next to her bed. She opened her closet and ruffled through the clothing hanging there. After settling on a white top and black jeans, she dressed herself. With purpose, she walked outside into the sun that had peeked through the clouds. A smile crossed her face as she settled into a deck chair to speak with her phone again.

BUT I WILL NOT USE THOSE WORDS (NOT ONE)

I have a dog. He is not like most dogs. He is not black and he is not white. But he comes to me and he sits with me. My dog and I talk. He gives me much joy when he talks to me.

At times we talk of things we do not see. These may be the best talks we have.

But there are times when my dog has no joy. He asks me if I do not see that he is not a real dog. And I say to him but you are a real dog. He asks me are you sure. I say I am but he goes on. I do not bark. I do not run and worst of all I have no tail.

So I hold him close and I say to him you are a dog if I say you are a dog. He smiles but he does not wag his tail. My dog has no tail.

I am in a group of three who write. One day we three sit. And we say we all can write. And we all say yes. Then one of us says let us write on this and on that. And I think I do not know how to write on this and I do not know how to write on that. I did at one time but now I do not know how to write.

But then I do. That night I get up from my bed and I walk down the stairs in the dark. I start to write. I turn it on and I start to type. Just like that. I do not think too much. I only type.

Then I tell my dog I have some lines and I read these lines to my dog. My dog says these are not just lines these are a real tale. I tell my dog these words and lines are short and these lines do not shine. But my dog says these lines are a tale if I say they are a tale.

My dog asks me if he can have the tale. I tell him he may have the tale but the tale is for my friends too. And my dog smiles.

We three sit one more time and you ask me to read my lines. You smile and clap and I have no fear. I say this is my tale. It may come up to you and it may say to you that it is not what it should be. All I can ask is for you to hold it close and tell it that it is a tale.

As I start to read I think I see a wag.

I have a dog. He is not like most dogs.

Just Hatched

Blue. Everything is blue. The sky is monochromatic from edge to edge. Down at the horizons it's a little paler, but the colour up above dazzles my eyes. My body's not moving, but somehow I'm suspended up here. I look down and understand it's water below me - water as far as I can see in every direction.

This must be a dream. But it feels too awake - I feel alive in a non-dreamlike way. This uncertainty is troubling – am I sleeping or not? I remember the tests for dreaming. Do the rules of normal life apply? If I shut my eyes and open them again does everything stay the same? Does any of this make sense?

I close and open my eyes once and then again, but nothing has changed. I'm up here in the blue. It can't be, but I know I'm really here. This is no dream.

The atmosphere comes up against my eyes and makes me blink. I'm moving. My ears are ringing with that small high-pitched buzz that comes with the quietest of silences, but over top of the whine there's a roar. The wind is growling past my face but it's muffled by something over my ears.

My body doesn't feel right. Somehow I'm inconsequential. There's no weight to me, I can feel it in my bones. I'm solid but I'm much too light – shouldn't be able to stay up here in the sky like this. I'm sure that's where I am.

I turn my head again and look in every direction. It's not all blue, there are greens and browns up ahead in the distance. That's an island. I must be over the ocean - there's too much water for this to be a lake, at least not the kind of lake I'm used to.

There's a scraping high scree of a sound that comes from the left of me. My first thought is how tuneless it sounds. Then it repeats and it starts to make sense. I can understand what it means. I scan across to the left and down and see a big bird passing me. He's a gull, a herring gull if I remember my bird book pictures correctly. Not sure how I knew it was a he though. But I know it as sure as I know...

But what do I know? I'm up here over the ocean heading for an island and a giant gull has just pulled alongside. He said something to me and for a moment I thought I understood him.

The big gull sings again. This time it's clear. He's telling me there is a beautiful updraft current just off the edge of that island. He's heading there and wants me to join him.

If a bird can talk to me, I suppose I can talk back. I'll tell him to shoo. I'm starting to enjoy this flying and I don't need some gull getting in my way.

I open my mouth to scare him off and the strangest sound comes out of me. It's more of a squawk than a word. I try again and the same grating noise results. The gull answers. He knows what I'm saying and he comments that I'm being antisocial – it's not the way of the flock.

I move my arm toward my mouth because it feels so dry. My lips feel stiff and I can't articulate the sounds I'm looking for. My arm comes across my field of view and there's something seriously wrong. It's a white wing covered in feathers. I stare in disbelief, stunned for the second it takes me to realize that now I'm falling.

I've been flying without thinking, on autopilot. My wings have been slowly moving up and down. I understand that now. But once I think about my arms... I mean my wings, this flying business gets a whole lot more complicated. Stretching my wing back out cuts the fall and I swoop back up into a safe and comfortable position.

But now that I'm aware of my wings, everything is different. I realize that there is some movement required to stay up here in the air. Birds... us birds can't just float along through the sky without any effort.

So I start from the basics. The movement I need comes mostly from the shoulder. Up and down, up and down. That keeps me aloft, but I need a little more subtlety to move forward. Somewhere deep inside I can understand that the wind has to be taken into consideration. It's coming from the left side and a little from the front. This requires a slightly different flexion of my elbows to keep me on an even keel.

I can feel that I need to move the feathers at my back end, my tail feathers. It's not a movement of the hips, it's a group of muscles that I didn't have last night and I just know that they tip my tail feather assembly from side to side.

After a few awkward dips and near-stalls, I'm starting to get the hang of things.

I can push hard for a few flaps and then hold my wings still. With a twist of the tail and a change of the angles up front I can execute spectacular dips and breathtaking turns.

I've always wanted to fly. Since I've been a child I've watched the birds and jealously wondered at their place in the world. I've been in airplanes, but that was never like this. The planes fight gravity and pound it into submission with slashing propellers and flame belching jets. The birds always seemed to work with the sky and together they flew. Today, I've realized my dream.

When I think of breath, I understand that there's something different about the way I'm breathing. The air comes into me like it did before, but now it's making its way deeper inside me. As well, I can feel that I'm not using the same muscles to move air as I did before. It's my wings that are doing the work. I lift them with the powerful muscles on either side of my keel and my chest is pulled open and the air rushes in. On the down flap I'm pushing that air from deep inside my abdomen and even in my bones out through my mouth.

I remember being told that I should breathe from down inside my belly. I always understood it was just an expression. The air used to only go as far as the bottom of my lungs and come back out. Now it's different; the air rushes into my lungs with each breath but it goes on further, into my belly and into my bones. I can sense a chill along my forearm or forewing or whatever I should call it as the air moves back and forth.

There are more birds around me now as I come in closer to the island. I'm understanding more and more of what they are saying. There are so many messages. They are telling us that certain parts of the land are taken, we shouldn't try landing there. There's a message that a big-black back is up above us and should be watched carefully. He's already killed one of my kind this morning. Some young birds are laughing as they go on about the great updraft at the interstice between the land and the sea. They understand that the warming of the air above the land meeting the constant temperatures over the ocean has caused an almost solid rising atmospheric column.

I look over and see a large group of birds sitting almost motionless on the rising air. The slight tips of their wings and tails keep them in the column and they slowly rise. When they reach the place where the air won't lift them anymore, they turn and fall into the open space. The young ones brag of how high they've risen and how far they will glide off into the ocean without effort. The older ones say nothing, but they rise higher and I can see they will drift farther.

I'll try this sometime, it looks like wonderful fun, but now I'm hungry. I've been flying a long time and I need food.

I have no idea what I can eat out here and I don't know where to start looking. Without thinking I start to speak – no, it's not speaking, it's singing. My song is simple "I'm hungry, I'm hungry." Yesterday it would have sounded like a tuneless squawk, but now I hear the beauty of my own voice and I can appreciate the harmonies around me that seemed cacophonous just a short while ago. There is a choir like none I've ever heard before with so many parts telling of the joy of flight and the details of survival.

I find myself lost in the music - it comes through me and there is nothing else I can think about. When I wake from the trance I'm slipping along low just at the edge of the water looking down to the bottom. There are sea urchins there and I know it's what I want.

I make a clumsy landing on the water above a fruitful bottom. With a quick push back of my legs I'm under the surface and there is an urchin in my beak. The time under the water is at once frightening and exhilarating. I stop and breathe heavily before I can work up the concentration to fly off somewhere safe with my meal.

The air above me punches into my back before the claws hit the side of my head. A big black-back is on top of me and I've dropped the food. All I can think of is that I must get out of here. I paddle hard with my feet and frantically lift my wings. I don't move fast, but the bigger gull isn't interested in me. He only wants my urchin.

It takes four flaps for me to gain the air and I don't look back until I'm over the land. I'm exhausted and I find a place to settle down away from the rest of the birds. I'm starting to understand them, but I know that I don't really fit in here.

Flying is only a part of this new life that I've woken to today. The rest, the majority of this altered existence, will be a brutish battle to survive. I notice that I have to work to breathe again. Here on the ground, my wings aren't pushing the air around - I need to work my chest like I did earlier today. Somehow it takes more effort now.

I'll explore a bit, just walk around and see where I've come to rest. These legs are so spindly, there's so little muscle to them. I can move, but it's awkward. It tires me just to go a few steps. I miss my old legs.

The wind blows hard, so I sit with my face into the gusts. It just comes naturally for me to do this. The wind smooths out my feathers and it feels like I'm back up in the air. But I know I can't fly all of the time, I have to rest.

I see a strangely shaped stick in front of me and I wonder what the back of it looks like. My first inclination is to reach out and turn it over but I remember I have no hands. Only these misshapen wings with no use other than flight and a set of legs fit only for inelegant walking. I miss my past, I'm cold and I'm alone.

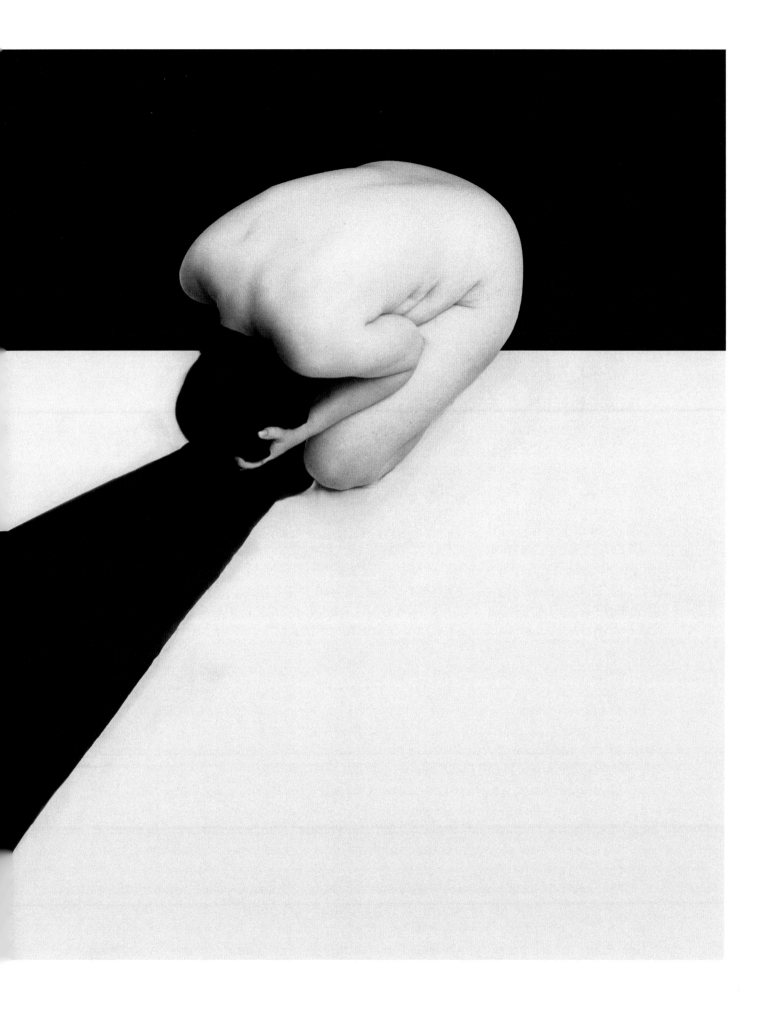

Rule of Thirds

1. The Nine Months

I hope I can remember all of this later, but something deep inside of me suggests that another chapter is coming and all of this will soon be gone.

Right now my memory is complete. Everything back to the very beginning is clear. I have always understood my home. Her words are clear and even when she doesn't speak, I understand her intent. The communication feels almost chemical.

He visited just before the beginning of everything and somehow I know of this. It doesn't make sense to have experienced something that occurred before I even was. But I know the memories are real and they are distinct.

Home complained of a bad headache, but he persisted. Seconds before I came into being, home commented that there was something out of place in the room. The visitor complained that everything was ruined, but he was wrong. I know the visit is what I came from.

How do I explain this experience from before my existence? I'm not clear about it, but it seems that parts of me came together that day and those parts had lives of their own before that. They were simpler than I am, but they had a primitive intelligence of some sort. I don't know why I have no memories from before the day of the visit, just a feeling that my parts must have had their own life before I came to be.

Life is grand. So little is asked of me. I float in a sustaining broth of a perfect warmth and experience the world. Constant temperature is important to me and home is nearly perfect. There are times when home is excited - I can tell that from the chemicals that flood me – and it gets just a bit too hot. It's really nothing I should complain about, but I would appreciate it if she would just stay calm and thermoregulate more conscientiously.

I've always been able to sense sound, but in the last month something has changed in my hearing ability. Noises from outside have become clearer. It's never been a problem to understand home and the visitor. Their sounds have been just outside since this all started. Home is always here and I'd estimate that the visitor is nearby for almost half of the time.

They speak to me and they speak to each other. There is something familiar about these two that lets me intuit their meaning when they make noise. It's only over the last short time that I've realized there are more like home and the visitor. They make noises more faintly, but I'm starting to understand what some of the others are meaning.

The noise seems to be about me and home. They comment on how proud home must be of me. I'm not really completely clear on the meaning of this, but it seems that it has to do with pleasure.

What more pleasure could I want? I float here without many distractions. The booming low frequency rhythm I hear comforts me endlessly. From the beginning that music has been here, I can't imagine existence without it. I don't think it's unfair to suggest that sound is a part of me.

The other sounds are more problematic. Home brings inanimate objects inside. They don't come right into my room, but they pass by and the burbling and wheezing is a distraction. There is movement of parts of home associated with these foreign bodies passing by, a squeezing and relaxation that upsets my sense of equilibrium. Every day this happens. If I could, I'd complain to whoever is running things.

I'm happy that I don't have to take anything inside myself. What an inefficient way to provide power. Home goes to great effort to prepare these foreign objects and then she sends them out. That business is even closer to me than the incoming. This involves more contractions and it's perhaps the most disturbing part of my life. It's happened since the start though, so I suppose it's necessary.

I should be grateful. Home has given me everything I need. This tube running from the centre of me brings liquid into me and then takes it back out after a course through my body. I suppose in that way, I'm not that much different than home. She does it all for me and there is no effort on my part.

My arms and legs are developing well. I've just discovered that by moving them I can change my position. Until this happened, I never thought about up and down. Now I understand that there is a way that I'm positioned that is a little more comfortable. But I can move my arms and legs and put myself into what I would call upside down. That's a funny concept and I'm not sure I can explain it clearly.

My latest adventure is moving my legs hard against the inside of home. When she's dormant it wakes her. The visitor laughs when I do this and I enjoy entertaining him.

There is nothing inside here beyond me. There are times when I think nothing else in the world matters. I've heard home and the visitor talk of love. When these conversations occur home floods me with the most pleasant of chemicals. I don't understand this, but perhaps some day I will. There may be adventures ahead I haven't dreamed of.

2. The Nine Decades

All things considered, it would be hard to complain about my life. I don't have clear memories of my earliest days, but I know they were times of self obsession. The world was made for me and nothing was more important than my happiness.

When I was young, days stretched out beyond the horizon. My friends and I never thought about what was coming next. Perhaps our attitude made the time dilate. Summers back then were longer than years are now. Life was less complicated. We would play outside on freezing winter days and only return home frostbitten when our mothers embarrassed us by hollering us in for supper.

In those days I was happy with everyone. My parents looked after me and my brothers were among my best friends. Outside of the home there was a code of fellowship between us. We knew we all had each other's backs and would never desert each other. But we didn't expect much from our friends - it was understood that we all wanted happiness, and as long as we made each other happy we were good.

Teenage years were more complex. Music was the first hint that something was changing. Rock and roll separated me from my parents. When I was a child, the family listened to mom and dad's music and it pleased us all.

But when the guitar driven, hip swinging noise born of teenage hormones came onto the television on Sunday nights, something changed. The drums drilled new ideas into all of our developing heads.

There was an element of danger to this music. Its rhythms spoke to us of discontent and the freedom of youth. And the message was framed by the possibility of doing something with a girl.

None of us understood what this was, but gradually, girls became more fascinating. They were foreign creatures. Most of them weren't interested in the games we played and they talked a different way than we did. They seemed closer than my friends and I, and they spent much of their time laughing at us.

Maybe it was their disdain that attracted us. My oldest and tallest friend was the first to have a girlfriend. As much as we pestered him, he wouldn't tell us anything about this new experience. It didn't take long for him to drift away from us. His idea of a good time changed in ways the rest of us couldn't fathom.

One by one the gang fell away, until all that was left was my younger brothers. My old friends would acknowledge me and when there weren't girls around it was like the old days. But it was obvious their priorities had changed.

My real interest in the other sex came on gradually. There was a girl in my class who spent too much time looking my way. I didn't respond at first because she seemed plain. Her face was too square, her hair was too short, and she wore glasses.

But her smile was something else and it wore me down. It wasn't long before I smiled back when she looked. We were both at the same school dance and somehow, we ended up on the floor together. I can't even remember who asked who.

It took three weeks before I kissed her and she suddenly became the most beautiful girl I had ever seen. I had a girlfriend, and we spent most of our time in each other's company. The kissing progressed and we found ourselves looking for empty rooms to enjoy the thrill of each other's touch. This was the first experience in my life that I didn't want to share with anyone else. It wasn't important for anyone to know what we were doing. The two of us were enough.

That lasted about a year and then I found my life partner. At first, she wasn't much different than the other girl, but gradually we both knew we had something special. We fell in love. In the early days neither of us really understood what that meant or could truly believe that the other felt the same way, but our feelings deepened.

By the time we decided to marry, we both realized that we were going to be together for life. The first years were easy, the thrill of having someone always on your side was something I hadn't had since I was a young child. We became our own family and when the kids came everything solidified. There was no way out of this relationship and we never looked for reasons to quit.

Our three children made both of us understand more about the way our parents had felt about us. I suddenly recognized the depth of love and sacrifice that my mother and father had for me.

The kids grew up and all three of them moved away. We loved them dearly, but felt a relief at being alone together again. It seemed we had been a pair forever. It was hard to remember times before there was an us.

Our parents passed on and our children had children. The idea of family further evolved. It was difficult at first to understand the kids' new loyalties, but like us they seemed to appreciate us more as their own children grew.

We often talked about who would go first and when it was you, I knew I'd had enough.

3. The Nine Days

I don't understand why my memories of the past are so vague. I know I fell down and was brought to the hospital, but the details are foggy. The family came to visit me and eight days ago they decided to remove all life support.

There's something about this existence that feels familiar. It seems that I've been here before. I'm floating inside something and the outside world is separated by some impermeable border.

I remember seeing, smelling, and feeling. Those are all different now, but the memories are as good as the real sensations. My body is still here, but it isn't that much use. I can sense the pounding of my heart and it's obvious that its intensity is decreasing.

The one positive thing about all of this is how little effort it takes to keep going. I do have to breathe a little. Perhaps once a minute, that's enough to keep me here. It is getting more difficult to the point where I wonder if it's worth all the effort.

Beyond the breathing, there's nothing I have to do. I remember them putting tubes into me and they supplied most of what I needed. Nutrition, fluids, and a little extra oxygen all came in through the lines. The tubes made me happy, but there was a familiarity that confused me a little.

I can still hear. No doubt this would surprise everyone who has come to visit as much as it amazes me. Everything sounds like it's underwater, but I know who comes into my room and I hear everything they say.

It takes some effort to understand all of the conversations, but I have nothing else to do, so I invest considerable effort into putting everything together.

It's been a long time since I've felt this alone. The kids and grandchildren come to my room and talk with each other. Occasionally they will say something to me, but it's obvious that they don't think I can understand.

They had a long conversation around my bed about shutting off the tubes. When my daughter told them they shouldn't speak so loudly, both of my sons insisted that it was obvious I couldn't hear or understand anything they said.

Still, I have to agree with them that shutting things down was the best decision.

120

I know there is no future for me here and I'm actually eager to find out what is next. Since my wife died, a big part of me has been looking forward to the possibility of reconnecting with her in some way.

The part of this that hurts and gives me so much joy at the same time is when the kids come in alone. Invariably they hold my hand and talk to me. I think the fact that they don't think I can hear them makes them completely honest. Perhaps they are telling the truth in ways that they can't even manage inside their own heads.

They all say pretty well the same thing. They love me, they appreciate how much their mother and I did for them and they are sad that I am leaving their lives. The pain of this is that I can't answer. I want to squeeze their hands and sit up and hug them. I wish I could tell them how much I love them and how I know what they feel about me.

I also wish I could explain how little I am worried about finishing up. There are things I gradually came to understand as I aged that are completely clear to me now. Life is finite. It seems such an obvious thing to say now, but I'm not sure I really understood in my younger days.

The real joys of life are about relationships with other people. The bookends of my life have been alone. We all start and end by ourselves, but the meat of our existence is the time we spend with other people.

Starting life with my parents was just a preview of the possibilities of interactions with others. Family and friends are what life is all about. I understand now that growing up and maturing is about seeing others. In my life this truth became clearer to me as I got older.

I lie here and it seems I'm floating in a fluid broth that keeps me alive. I understand enough of my situation and simple biology to realize that there is no real liquid that I'm in.

I'm soon moving on and yet a part of me will go on in those I've interacted with throughout my life. My existence at this point is mostly about memory and when I go, it will all be memory. The only difference is that the memories will reside inside someone else's head.

The cycle is nearly finished and I'm satisfied with the ride I've been on. I have learned as much as I could manage and I'm sure now that I've been able to sort out the really useful bits from the mundane. Everything I learned in school and in my work was really only pointing me in the direction of more important truths.

The world will go on and my memories and even some of my genetics will still be there. I'm happy to be a memory and know that this means so much more than anyone in the room can understand.

Acknowledgements

Andrew

First thanks must go to Kaleigh for her wonderful photographs. From the first time I saw her work at Oceanview Art Gallery, I was impressed by her exceptional vision and masterful technique. It is a thrill to collaborate with such a talented artist.

Thank you to Tammy Wrice and Michelle Penny Rowe for their partnership in the creation of Authors in Art. This unique event which pairs some of the finest visual artists and writers in Newfoundland was an early inspiration for the book.

Many of the stories in Bifocal started as projects with the Freshwater Writers' Circle. I'm grateful to Jesse Bown, Pat Collins, Angie Green, Dorothy Harvey, Marylynne Middelkoop, and Chris Tompkins for their inspiration and direction.

Heartfelt appreciation to Matt LeDrew of Engen Books for his interest in the project and to Ali House and Matthew Daniels for their sensitive and accurate editing. Thank you to Heather Benoit for her early reading of the book.

A sincere thank you to David and Dawn for sharing the parts of their histories that inspired stories.

None of this would have ever happened without the support and encouragement from my best friend and first reader, Ingrid.

Kaleigh

This project began in 2015 after the first Authors in Art event hosted by Oceanview Art Gallery in Freshwater, NL. It featured authors and visual artists who were given the chance to make interpretations of each other's work. Andrew had a vision for the kind of book this idea could unearth, and we partnered with visions of the unique space it could create. All art has a story, a soul its own and to see the same face through two lenses is compelling.

Thank you, Andrew, for seeing the potential in an evening of art and trusting me to be your partner in this endeavor. You have made this a genuine partnership. Thank you for finding new ways to tell and interpret stories.

Thank you to Engen Books for valuing our stories, for going on this journey with us to bring Bifocal forth into the world, and for cherishing and cheerleading your creators. I'm so thankful for this opportunity to work together and for all you do to foster creativity.

My parents, Mike and Marylynne, have always been the most supportive of my crazy ventures. From staying up late to help me sew a ballgown, or gutting a piano to set on fire, there was never a shortage of helping hands. They taught me to be brave in the face of choosing my own path and to venture into the world with kind eyes and a strong spirit. Thank you, mom, thank you, dad - I'm so proud to be your daughter.

My husband, Matthew has been helping me with photos for years, but more than any ladder he's hung over, he has valued me deeply, regardless of accomplishment. When it feels like inspiration may never return, he replenishes my dampened spirit and loosens the grip I have on the elusive muse. Thank you, Matthew, you are the love of my life and it's a gift to build our life together.

To the featured models in this book:

Drew Saurus, thank you for your no-questions-asked kind of help. We all need a friend like you. You truly are one of the greatest artistic facilitators I have encountered, and you are so appreciated. There are few else I'd trust to hold a flaming hoop of fire for the sake of a photo.

Janine O'Rielly, photoshoots with you become performance pieces as you embody each role. It's a thrill to get to create with you. In the accompanying image to "Paint", Janine is the model and artist who created the masterpiece painted on her skin.

Josh Driscoll, your light shines strong in each step you take. Thank you for encouraging, helping, and supporting me in all things. You taught me the importance of perseverance and gentleness in the face of it.

Brittney Power, my oldest friend and the one who's always made me feel comfortable being entirely me. Thank you for a friendship steeped in imagination, acceptance, and adventure. I'm so lucky to have snagged a friend as incredible as you so early.

Zoe Vail, one of my younger muses but no less eager to leap into her roles. Zoe Love, thank you, and never let your shining spirit wane. "

Biographies

ANDREW PEACOCK was born in Toronto and raised in the town of Kapuskasing in northern Ontario. After finishing degrees in biology at Trent University and veterinary medicine at the University of Guelph he moved with his wife to the small fishing village of Freshwater on the island of Newfoundland. As a veterinarian he worked in a mixed animal practice from 1982 until 2010. Andrew and his wife also established and ran the independent bookstore Waterwords in Carbonear.

His book Creatures of the Rock was published by Doubleday Canada in 2014. It was long listed for the 2015 Leacock Medal for Humour and won the Newfoundland and Labrador Books Award for the best non-fiction book of 2015. In 2017 the Vancouver Island Libraries Board included Creatures of the Rock in its list of the 150 books Canadians should read.

In 2019 his children's book, *One Brave Boy and his Cat*, was released from Flanker Press with art by Angie Green.

In 2020 his pandemic thriller, *VIRAL*, was released from Engen Books.

KALEIGH MIDDELKOOP is a photographer who primarily uses self-portraiture as a means to tell stories and express ideas. Heavily influenced by fairy tales and the slightly strange, her work has surreal and magical elements woven throughout. She is always exploring new ways to inspire imagination by making costumes and props for her images.

After spending her formative years in Newfoundland, Canada, she studied photography in Ontario at Algonquin College. Graduating in the top of her class, she has gone on to create immersive gallery shows featuring her photography, costumes, and props. In 2017 Kaleigh and her dog Winston moved to Indiana, USA, to be with her husband, Matthew.

Kaleigh is a featured artist at Bellazo in downtown Wabash, IN as well as Ocean View Art Gallery in Carbonear, NL.

Made in the USA
Middletown, DE
03 November 2021